Picture Love

A Good Bad Idea Story

A.F. ZOELLE

Copyright © 2021 A.F. Zoelle

www.afzoelle.com

All rights reserved.

This is a work of fiction. Names, characters, places, and incidents are products of the author's imagination or used fictitiously. Any resemblance to actual persons, living or dead, is purely coincidental. All products and brand names are registered trademarks of their respective holders/companies.

This book or any portion thereof may not be reproduced or used in any manner whatsoever without the express written permission of the publisher except for the use of brief quotations in a book review.

Cover Design by Adrijus of Rocking Book Covers

Editing by Pam of Undivided Editing

Proofreading by Sandra of One Love Editing

Layout by A.F. Zoelle of Sarayashi Publishing

ISBN: 978-1-954202-01-6

WELCOME TO SUNNYSIDE!

Immerse yourself in the world of interconnected series set in the fictional town of Sunnyside

Full of cute sweetness and sexy fun, every story ends with a satisfying HEA and no cliffhangers. Since all of the following series are set in the same town, you can expect to see cameos of your favorite characters! The books are funny, steamy, and can be read in any order.

Good Bad Idea: Romances featuring bad ideas that lead to true love. It starts with Rhys expecting to wake up hungover after his bachelor party—not married to his best man. His biggest surprise is falling in love with his new husband.

Suite Dreams: Couples fall in love at Luxurian Suites Hotels all over the world, starting with Jude and Rigby. Their meet-cute in an airport on a snowy day leads to a hotel room with only one bed and a happily ever after.

Author's Note

*The Good Bad Idea series can be read in any order. However, if you would like to see where Felix's story began, please refer to **Love Means More**. He also appears in Chapter 8 of **Fancy Love**, which includes the first mention of Arsène. This book starts a little over two weeks after the last chapter of **Love Directions**.*

Dedication

For everyone who needs a laugh right now, I hope Felix and Arsène brighten your spirits.

Chapter 1

Felix Muphy

As I stood in front of the Eiffel Tower, I was so glad I had been brave enough to come by myself to enjoy Paris. I had originally planned to go with my boyfriend, Danny, but I dumped his cheating ass last year. At first I thought it would be too pathetic to travel by myself, but my roommate, North, talked me into it.

I was early for my meeting with my friend Izzy's older brother, who had agreed to play tour guide for me over the next five days. He had shown me a couple of pictures of Arsène before I left. The man was so handsome that I wondered why he had a career behind the camera as a photographer instead of in front of it as a model. Clean-shaven, with a chiseled jaw and hazel eyes that lit a spark inside me, he was so beautiful I wasn't sure how I would keep my cool around him.

Izzy had warned me his brother was a bit of a player, which was normally an automatic no-go for me when I was all about being committed to my partner. However, it was time for me to stop thinking that being someone's boyfriend was the only way to enjoy being with a man.

There were plenty of beautiful bachelors with sexy accents in Paris for me to play with on my vacation. There was one tiny problem standing in my way, though:

it was hard to hit on a Frenchman when I didn't speak the language. Anything beyond *oui, non, pardon,* and *parlez-vous anglais* proved my high school French class was a wasted effort.

My great idea was to ask a gorgeous Parisian guy to take a selfie with me to post on social media to make my asshole ex jealous. However, the fatal flaw was that none of them would give me and my shitty French the time of day. It annoyed me how hot it was when they sneered at me as they walked past me. How was it fair they could make ignoring me sexy?

After my fifth rejection, I was ready to give up on my stupid idea when I saw a god of a man approaching. His navy blazer had the sleeves rolled up to reveal his beautiful forearms, with a hint of a floral pattern on the cuffs that matched his pocket square. The jacket's cut emphasized his masculine shoulders and tiny hips. He kept it casual by pairing it with a white undershirt and skinny jeans, but his aristocratic features elevated the look into elegance. The best part was he had just the right amount of scruff to inspire dirty thoughts about it brushing against my thighs while giving me a sinfully delightful blow job. *Fuck.*

At the sight of my jaw on the ground because of how goddamn gorgeous he was, he quirked an eyebrow up at me. I wanted to kiss the smirk off his handsome face, then fall to my knees and worship his cock until he came. *Double fuck.*

If he wasn't going to ignore me, I might as well shoot my shot since I still had some time before I met up with

Arsène. I tried to sound confident when I asked, "*Parlez-vous anglais?*"

He grinned as he replied in accented English, "You ask that like you have rudely been told 'no' by several Parisians."

I rubbed the back of my head. "In their defense, I'm very aware that I'm an awful American because I only speak one language."

"That just makes you a normal American, *non?*"

I had to laugh at that. "Touché."

"Ah, see? You speak a little French after all. There is hope for you yet."

"Good to know," I said, grinning.

"So, what is your question?"

I felt like an idiot when I requested, "Would you take a selfie with me?"

"You want a stranger in your picture?"

It sounded stupid when he put it that way. "My ex is an asshole, so I wanted to make him jealous by taking pictures with a hot guy while I'm here. It's the least I can do to get some payback after he cheated on me."

The man stroked his chin as he mulled over my plight. "I see."

"He thinks I haven't moved on since I haven't dated anyone after we broke up last year." It was hard not to fidget under his hazel gaze that filled me with a chaotic mix of reactions ranging from horny to unusually nervous. "I hate how he gloats that I'm still single like it has anything to do with not being over him."

There was no judgment in his tone when he asked, "Have you actually moved on?"

"Absolutely. I'd never take him back after what he did to me."

"Ah, so you believe a little revenge is good for the soul?"

I couldn't tell if he was making fun of me or not, so I shrugged. "It helps."

He nodded to himself as he decided. "Very well. I will agree on one condition."

If he requested a hookup as payment, he was so hot that I'd consider it, preferences for commitment be damned. "Which is?"

"I am also allowed to take a picture of you with a real camera."

That was it? There had to be a catch. I looked at him suspiciously. "With my clothes on or off?"

The deep rumble of his laughter made heat pool in my belly. I wished I was a comedian so I could make him laugh all the time. "You should be careful making that kind of offer. It is tempting to say *oui* to both."

Lust rocketed through my system that someone as sexy as him would possibly be interested in seeing my scrawny ass. My mouth never knew when to quit while it was ahead, so I asked, "What's stopping you?"

His amusement turned his eyes into liquid gold that melted me into a puddle. "You will hardly think I am a gentleman if I try to get you naked before holding up my end of the bargain."

I bit my tongue to stop myself from volunteering to get naked anytime he wanted me to. "Fair enough."

"What kind of selfie were you hoping for?" A soft swear escaped me when he wrapped his arm around my shoulder to pull me into an embrace. "I guess the better question is, how jealous do you wish to make your ex?"

I swallowed hard as my heart hammered. That close, I could smell his cologne, which was dark and woodsy in a way that gave me the strangest urge to lick him. If I didn't get a handle on my hormones, I was going to embarrass myself something fierce. "What would you suggest?"

"Will a picture of us like this be enough? Perhaps a kiss on the cheek will do more, *non*?"

Was he serious? Could I be that lucky? "I like the way you think." Taking out my phone, I held it up to take a snapshot as the man of my dreams did as he promised. I was glad there would be photographic evidence of the moment, because otherwise, I'd assume it had all been an incredible dream. Then again, if it had been a dream, he wouldn't have been kissing me only on the cheek.

I pulled up the image to inspect it. The petty bastard in me gloated it would piss off Danny that such a sexy guy was showing interest in me. I couldn't wait to post it on social media and rub it in his face.

"Hmm, it is good, but I think we can do better. Perhaps a video this time?"

If he was volunteering to kiss me again, I was more than happy to accept. "Is that okay?"

"*Oui.*" The only thing sexier than his accent was him speaking French—even if it was only one word.

I hit the Start button as I held my arm out, saying a silent prayer that my shaking hand wouldn't fuck up the recording. I didn't resist as he reached over and guided my chin to turn toward him to claim my lips.

My world exploded into fire as he gave me the single best kiss of my entire life. He teased me with tenderness, before delving in for a taste as I opened for him.

I held on to him with my free hand as he made me weak in the knees with his passion. Melting against him with a moan, I surrendered to him. There was no hiding the fact that I was rock-hard and eager for more. It was impossible to worry about it when he was dominating my desires like he wanted to make me his. Everything in me was screaming, *Take me!*

He murmured something in French against my lips I hoped like hell translated to "Let's go back to my place and do this with our clothes off."

In a daze, I stopped the recording and stared up at him with a mix of shock and desperate need.

"You should check the video," he casually suggested, as if he hadn't just rocked my world.

It took an epic effort to release him and remember how to operate my phone to replay us making out in front of the Eiffel Tower. *City of Love, indeed.*

I awkwardly shifted and tried to disguise my hard-on without being glaringly obvious. My dick ached for attention as I enjoyed reliving the best moment of my life.

Knowing Danny would seethe with rage when he saw it made it even better. "*Wow.*"

"That should do nicely, eh?"

I laughed. "That's an understatement. He's going to die of jealousy when he sees this."

"He deserves far worse for cheating on someone as cute as you."

His compliment brought a blush to my cheeks. "Thanks." I mourned when he stepped away from me to put distance between us.

"I am curious. What will you call your sexy Parisian lover? Hopefully, something better than Pierre or Jacques."

"Am I not allowed to use your real name?" Damn, North would be so proud of me for making out with a guy before I even knew who he was. That was a move straight out of his playboy handbook.

"You can. But perhaps to you I am sexier as a Jean-Paul than a Michele."

Belatedly remembering my upcoming meeting with Izzy's brother, I was dazed enough to suggest his. "Would you object to Arsène?"

He grinned roguishly, making me fucking *swoon*. "Consider me impressed. Your poker face is quite good. You had me convinced you did not recognize me."

I blamed my confusion on the fact that all my blood was rushing down south, fueling my still-raging erection. "Huh?"

"I am Arsène Devereaux." Too many things were happening for me to process his words when our palms touched. He brought my hand up to kiss the back of it while holding my gaze, electrifying every nerve in my body as I trembled with lust. My poor dick was going to explode at this rate. "*Enchanté*, Monsieur Felix Murphy."

With his scruff, he looked like a totally different person from the pictures Izzy had shown me before I left. Not only did it make him unrecognizable to me but also a million times hotter. And now that I knew what a great kisser he was, I was in deep trouble. *Triple fuck.*

In true me fashion, I made a bigger ass of myself as I gawked at him. "Shit, Izzy's going to kill me."

"Why?"

"For kissing you."

Arsène gave me a serious case of blue balls as he ran his thumb over his lower lip while giving me a heated look. "Actually, I kissed you."

"I kissed you back!"

He licked his lips, sending my hormones into overdrive. "You certainly did. Quite well, I might add."

And I want to do it again—again and again and again forever. Thank god I had enough sense to keep that thought in my damn head.

Despite not saying it, he smirked like he knew exactly what I was thinking. "Did my brother explicitly say I was off-limits?"

"No, but he said you were a flirt."

His wicked smile did nothing to lessen the throbbing need I still suffered from. "He says as if he is any different." It was true, especially when teasing our mutual friend and his roommate, Wren. How those two hadn't fucked yet continued to baffle everyone in our group. "Devereaux men are notorious for being good flirts and even better lovers."

Quadruple fucking fuck. If he didn't stop, I was going to make an embarrassing mess of my pants. "Is that so?"

"Did he warn you to not find out for yourself?" The predatory look in his eyes made me want to say fuck it all and offer myself up to him. "I promise I only bite if you want me to."

It was a challenge to hold in my shameless plea for him to have his wicked way with me. I reminded myself that Izzy had cautioned me for a reason. As a relationship-only kind of guy, I was fundamentally incompatible with Arsène, who was only interested in having a good time.

But fuck if I wasn't dying for a chance at no-strings-attached sex with a gorgeous man like him who probably had the talent to back up his ego. Would it really be so wrong to end my dry spell after being left unsatisfied by my shitty ex? A relationship between me and Arsène could never work because of the ocean between us and the sizable age gap, so maybe I wouldn't fall into my normal trap. In theory, he was the perfect guy to show me how to have fun without ruining things by wishing for a commitment from my partner.

Faced with my silence, he commented, "It seems we are similar in ignoring Isidore's warnings about each other."

It was so strange hearing Izzy called by his first name when we all referred to him by his nickname. "He warned you about me?" Out of all our friends, I wasn't the one who required a warning label. "What did he say?"

"That I should behave myself with you." His impish smirk made me long to feel his lips on mine once more. "Luckily for us, he neglected to specify *how* I should behave. We will have much more fun that way."

Me and my hard-on *really* hoped he meant between the sheets later. "It sounds like we'll get along great, then."

The pleasure he derived from my response had me ready to invite him back to my hotel room. If I had been North, I would have. But I wasn't that bold or smooth of a player. I was lucky I could speak in full sentences in the face of his immense sexiness and powerful pheromones.

"I am sure of it. To start things off, what do you say to going up the Eiffel Tower? It would be an excellent opportunity for more photographs. Afterward, we can stop for lunch."

If he meant more pictures where we got to make out, I was down for that. "Sounds great. Lead the way."

I might have let him walk ahead to sneak a peek at perfection. Who could blame me? I was only human, and his tight ass was made for ogling—and hopefully groping if things went well.

Chapter 2

Arsène Devereaux

When Isidore first asked me to play tour guide for one of his friends, I had refused. I was a busy man with a fantastic career as a famous fashion photographer. Taking an American brat around tourist traps was not how I wished to spend my limited free time.

At my job, the most beautiful men in the world surrounded me. I had my choice of handsome gentlemen to enjoy whenever I was in the mood. They were all self-assured, egotistical guys who demanded to be worshipped, which I was happy to do for an evening of pleasure.

Of course, there were exceptions like Rune Tourneau, whom I had met before either of us had become famous. The moody intellectual with a face and body to die for had been a fun change of pace when I was in the rare mood to let someone dominate me. It had been years since we had been together in bed, but I still had a fondness for him and his gentle, down-to-earth nature and acerbic wit. Our amorous interest had faded to friendship, which was its own gift.

Isidore had sent me a picture to tempt me into helping his American friend with his first solo trip abroad. It had been a candid shot of an amused Felix. He was a lanky kid, with prominent cheekbones and delicate eyebrows. I saw a hint of his green eyes that beckoned me for a closer look. His tousled hair caused me to think inappropriate things about a twenty-two-year-old. Cute was not something I indulged in, but Felix's angelic face and devilish smile were an interesting contradiction that drew me to him. I consented to my brother's request, hoping there would be some fun in it for me.

Knowing my voracious sexual appetite, Isidore had warned me to be careful with Felix and not break his heart. Given how easy it had been to tempt him into a kiss, I had no worries about him being the falling-in-love type. If he was open to having a good time, I was more than willing to show him one.

The way he kissed me back told me he was not nearly as innocent as his face led me to believe. It also left me hungry for another taste, not to mention eager to get him into my studio for a clothing-optional photo shoot after he volunteered.

My gaze traveled over him as I stood beside him on the highest viewing platform of the Eiffel Tower. His sense of awe and wonder was sweet. Having lived in Paris my entire life, the place did not hold the same appeal to me as it did to foreigners who romanticized it as the City of Love. It was home, nothing more.

It was precious watching him snapping a million pictures with his phone. He was much more interesting to study than the landscape. In ripped jeans and an old band T-shirt, he was a far cry from the fussy, fashion-conscious models I dealt with in my line of work. Yet, his boyish good looks tempted me all the same.

He slid his mobile in his back pocket as he rested his forearms on the banister to drink in the city's view. I regretted not bringing my camera, because his smile was worthy of being photographed with proper equipment.

Felix drew me from my thoughts when he happily sighed. "It's so beautiful here."

Never taking my eyes off him, I agreed, "It is." I had never seen the appeal of boyish charm, but he was causing me to reconsider my stance.

"What's your favorite place in the city?"

"My studio."

His attempt at a stern look was adorable. "Your favorite *famous* place."

It was too much fun to tease him. "My studio *is* famous."

"You really are like your brother. He does that kind of deliberately obtuse shit all the time."

I grinned. "Where do you think he learned it from?"

"Oh, so *you're* the bad influence."

"So bad that I am good," I said with my most charming smile. My words sent a visible shiver through him. *Excellent.*

"I'll bet."

I cut him a break. "To answer your question, the Louvre is my favorite famous place that I do not own."

"Can we go there sometime this week?"

"Of course. I am quite familiar with it. We can plan a schedule over lunch."

"I'd love that. Is Notre Dame far from here?"

I pointed to it in the distance. "A bit. It is about a five-kilometer walk from here, so taking a taxi might be best."

It did not surprise me when he used his phone to convert the measurements. "Oh, so about three miles. Yeah, that makes sense. We can see more doing that."

"As you wish."

"There's so much to see, I have to keep reminding myself I don't have to do it all in one day. But five days doesn't feel like enough time to enjoy everything."

"Why did you choose to visit Paris?"

"Originally, I was supposed to come here last year with my ex, Danny. I thought he wanted to propose to me in the City of Love, like in the movies. He was *obsessed* with the cinema." Felix sighed as he ruffled his brunet hair, making it stand up in adorable spikes. "It all fell apart when I discovered he was cheating on me. I was such an idiot. But I was so excited about our trip, I didn't want to give it up just because I dumped him. It took me longer to save up the money to come since we wouldn't be splitting the costs, but it feels good to be here without him. My only regret is that I was stupid enough to fall in love with such an asshole."

Without meaning to, I reached out to rub his back in comfort. "Do not be too hard on yourself, eh? You are still young. Experience only comes with age and mistakes."

"The shitty thing is my brother, Augie, tried to warn me that Danny was a douchebag. But I thought he was being overprotective, as per usual. I don't understand why I keep trying to prove him wrong when all he ever does is look out for me. I hate that I'm his stupid kid brother who always needs rescued. You'd think I'd know better, but nope, I'm just a dumbass."

"It is an older brother's job to protect his younger siblings. If younger brothers did not get up to mischief, older brothers would be very bored."

He gave me a knowing look. "I'm sure Izzy gave you hell."

"The ocean between us has changed nothing in that regard. The troublemaking is merely long-distance now."

"I should have guessed right away you two were related. You have the same regal air he does. We used to tease him about being a prince in disguise trying to live the quiet life of the commoner."

The thought made me chuckle. "What does that make me? Prince Charming?"

Heat colored his cheeks, but he continued playing the game. "Maybe. Maybe not."

"Are you playing coquettish to win my favor?"

"No—well, I mean, I want you to like me—not like, *romantically*, but like as in *like*-like me—because if you don't, this week is going to be awkward as fuck."

Unable to resist, I cupped his flushed cheek in my palm, brushing my thumb against it. "You have nothing to worry about. I would not have kissed you if I did not like you."

His green eyes went wide with shock. They were the color of pale jade and utterly entrancing. I could not wait to photograph him. His lips parted, filling me with a need to claim them once more in a heated kiss. My reaction to him puzzled me. I barely knew him, plus he was my brother's age. A pretty face alone was not enough to justify my interest. But for some odd reason, I felt an almost magnetic pull in his direction.

"But you don't even know me."

"We have all week to learn about each other."

His eyelashes fluttered as he looked up at me. "Um, I didn't say it before, but I appreciate you being willing to show me around when you're so busy. I'm sure entertaining an American kid in your free time isn't your idea of fun."

"And yet, I am already enjoying myself."

He seemed stunned by my admission. "Really?"

"*Oui.* Perhaps we should take another picture?"

He bit his lower lip, drawing my attention to them once more. "Is that okay?"

"*Absolument.*" I was curious what kind of photo he would ask for, while secretly hoping he asked to kiss again.

He moved to stand on my opposite side and nestled against me like he belonged there. I wrapped an arm around him and hugged him close. The sense of rightness I experienced holding him in my embrace was unexpected.

"Am I, um, allowed to—"

"Whatever you wish." I sincerely hoped he would take me up on that invitation.

He gave me a sweet kiss on the cheek as he snapped a selfie of us. I was used to ardent passion, not tenderness, so it set off an unfamiliar flutter within me. Rather than stir my desire, it made me hug him tighter. What an inexplicable reaction.

Felix snuggled against my shoulder, so I pressed my lips against his forehead in return. It earned me the cutest little gasp before a slight furrow in his brow replaced his surprise.

Perhaps I had pushed too far. "Should I not have done that?"

"No, that was sweet. Sorry, don't mind me. I'm just fighting a war with myself."

I arched an eyebrow at the unexpected answer. "About?"

"Part of me wants to be selfish, but the other part of me feels weird about it now that I know you're Izzy's brother." It was refreshing how he always said what he thought.

I stroked under his chin, making him tremble. "Ah, so you are wishing for me to kiss you again but do not feel you may ask."

The fire in his eyes sent a shocking explosion of lust inside me. "Actually, *I* want to kiss *you* this time."

While I preferred to be the one in control, there was something thrilling about him trying to dominate me. "What is stopping you?"

"Someone like you would never want to be kissed by me."

"*Au contraire.* I would enjoy that very much."

His jaw dropped in disbelief. "Seriously? *Why?*"

"I am curious about what kind of kiss you yearn to give me."

Felix delighted me when his answer came in the form of tugging on my shirt to bring me down to his level. He sucked on my lower lip before teasing me with a hint of tongue. When I tried to take control, he switched to little kisses that made me burn for more. I pressed him against the railing, cupping my hand around the back of his neck as I slid my tongue into his mouth. My prick stirred with desire when he laced his fingers through my hair to pull me closer with a breathy moan. I was consumed by a fiery need to have him under me, begging me for more as I showed him pleasures beyond his wildest dreams.

I drew back only because I was in danger of my arousal betraying me, but he did not release his hold on me. It was tempting to dive in for another taste of him when he licked his lips while looking up at me with an expression pleading for more. I was more than ready to bring him to my place and show him a good time.

To my surprise, he started laughing hard. I did not understand the source of his amusement, but the sight of his uninhibited joy suffused me with a warm glow. "What is so funny?"

"Sorry, I might have gotten so caught up in getting to kiss you I forgot about the picture."

I moved my hand to tip his chin back, stroking his jaw with my thumb. His smooth skin was baby soft. "Did you actually forget, or is it a convenient excuse to kiss me again so you may have another chance at a photo?"

His unrepentant grin was endearing. It was invigorating how he refused to be bashful and back down. "Probably a little of both."

"Perhaps we should get lunch first," I suggested. "There is a great place on the way to the Arc de Triomphe."

"If you're offering me a second shot, I guess I didn't do too badly, huh?"

I could not resist the urge to tease him. "You did well enough to make me reconsider whether a camera needs to be involved at all next time."

He placed a soft kiss under my chin that stirred unknown things inside of me. "Maybe you'll get lucky if lunch is good."

I wrapped my arm around his shoulder with a laugh as I guided him toward the exit. For a day I had expected to be an arduous chore, it was turning out to be a genuine delight.

FELIX MOANED AS HE finished his dessert after lunch. I shifted in my chair as the sound of it gave my body ideas about other ways I could inspire him to make such a sensuous noise. It had been a test of willpower, sitting across from him and watching him savor every bite of his meal. The sight of him in a near-euphoric state gave me visions of him under me as I sent him to a new height of sexual ecstasy.

Clearing my throat, I tried to refocus my attention on less amorous activities. "I am glad you enjoyed lunch."

"This was *amazing*, even though you ordered

escargot to gross me out. The joke's on you because I loved it."

"I was merely attempting to expand your culinary horizons."

"Uh-huh, sure. You *totally* didn't order it because you wanted to feel superior to me being too American to eat snails." He snorted in amusement.

"Perhaps it was a test to determine how adventurous you are."

He rested his chin on his hand while giving me a flirtatious look. It did nothing to abate my desire to add my bedroom as a stop on our Paris tour. "That seems like a strange method to judge how adventurous I am in bed. Is there some French expression about eating snails meaning you're into kinky stuff that I'm unaware of?"

Rather than answer, I drank my wine. "You are quite the tease, Monsieur Felix."

"Oh, and you're not?" He scoffed. "Please, you're a bigger flirt than my roommate, North."

"What can I say? I enjoy living life to the fullest."

"And I love getting into trouble, so it sounds like we might have some real fun together." He raised his wineglass in a toast to me.

"I will do whatever I can to ensure your stay here is enjoyable." I clinked my glass against his, and we both took a sip in celebration.

His cheeky grin once again made me regret not bringing my camera. "Including giving me a personal guided tour of your bedroom? I'm pretty sure that's going above and beyond what's necessary."

"Perhaps it is unnecessary, but it would be pleasurable." It became more and more tempting the longer I spent with him. His playfulness brought out that side of me which had gone into hiding because of how hard I worked without a break. I used to relax by indulging in beautiful men, but even that had lost its charm at some point. Felix was something entirely new and different.

"Don't tempt me," he warned with a laugh. "You're way too hot for me to put up anything but the barest resistance before I give in to you."

"Then I guess it is a good thing that the idea of you giving yourself to me brings me great pleasure. I would take *excellent* care of you."

There was a slight flush in his cheeks that had nothing to do with the wine he was drinking. "Oh, I'm sure of it."

"Your wish is my command."

I did not expect him to crack up at that. "Don't say that. It makes you sound like a sex genie who will grant my wildest wishes in bed if I rub you the right way—and I'm not talking about your lamp."

It was impossible to restrain myself from chuckling along with him. "Then that is good, since it is not my lamp I would wish you to rub."

He took a huge gulp of wine. "I'm warning you: if you keep teasing me, I'm going to get the wrong impression."

"I disagree. It sounds like you are getting the right idea."

"You're not interested in me, though."

I gave him a sensual look that made him flush to the tips of his ears. "Do not be so certain of that."

"Oh, lord." He finished his drink in a long swig. "I'm not sure if I'm going to survive five days of your teasing."

"Be brave, *mon ami*. The fun is only getting started." And I had every intention of having the best time possible.

Before we left the restaurant to go to the Arc de Triomphe, I went to the toilet. After finishing and washing my hands, I checked my phone. There was a text from my younger brother.

> **Isidore:** *I knew you would think Felix was cute, but kissing him, Arsène? Really? He's barely been in Paris a few hours.*

Despite being an ocean away, I could imagine his elegant eyebrow cocked at me in silent challenge. However, I refused to feel badly about my actions when I had done nothing wrong.

> **Arsène:** *Why do you seem surprised when he is as adorable as you promised?*

> **Isidore:** *What part of don't break his heart did you not understand?*

Arsène: *He is in no danger. The pictures were merely for show.*

Isidore: *I didn't realize I had to warn you, too.*

I puzzled over his message, but I could not figure out what he meant.

Arsène: *What are you talking about? You did warn me.*

Isidore: *Yes, not to break HIS heart. I didn't think I'd have to tell you to keep YOURS out of the equation.*

I shook my head at such a ridiculous notion. As a man who freely indulged in pleasure, I had never been tied down by anyone before. I was not about to change that, let alone for a mere kid.

Arsène: *What makes you think my heart would get involved?*

Isidore: *Because he's Felix.*

Arsène: *I do not understand what that would have to do with it.*

Isidore: *I hope you don't have to find out the hard way.*

I furrowed my eyebrows as I tried to decipher what he was saying. My brother's words only confused me further.

Arsène: *Meaning?*

Isidore: *Be careful.*

Arsène: *About what?*

Isidore: *Playing with fire.*

Arsène: *I do not have time to solve one of your riddles. Say what you wish to say.*

Isidore: *It's all or nothing with Felix. If you aren't willing to give everything up to love him with all of your heart, then don't play this game. You'll both end up heartbroken.*

Arsène: *Your worries are unfounded.*

Isidore: *For now. Try to keep it that way.*

There was something ominous about his words. It was a mystery to me why my brother would issue such a dire warning. For someone like me who had never bothered with love, it was absurd that he would think I would fall for Felix.

I returned to the dining room, where the man in question sat, smirking at his mobile screen as he typed a response. Taking my seat once more, I studied him as I tried to piece together what Isidore had been talking about. Between his cute face and his vivacious personality, Felix was quite lovable. But that did not translate to me falling *in* love with him. What was my brother so worried about?

Felix glanced up at me with a devious expression that stirred something inside me. "It worked."

"What did?"

"Our plan." He passed me his mobile to show me.

It was a picture of our kiss in front of the Eiffel Tower. I admired his natural eye for framing the photograph of us before reading the comments below it.

Northish: *Damn, you already found the hottest guy in Paris and made out with him? I'm so fucking proud of you, man. Hell yeah!*

Westie: *Wooooow, I don't know who is more gorgeous! When you're done sucking face with that sex god, can you find out if he has a sibling for me to play with? I'd love to practice my French (kissing) ^_~*

Wrenfair: *Dude, are all the men in Paris that hot? If they are, I'm booking the next flight over there.*

Izzily: *@Wrenfair I can assure you they are not. You have enough Parisians in your life as it is.*

Wrenfair: *@Izzily None that want to kiss me like that unless you're hiding a deep dark secret about wanting to secretly make out with me?*

Izzily: *@Wrenfair In your dreams.*

Wrenfair: *@Izzily Come on, that was ONE TIME. God, I moan your name in my sleep ONCE and you never let me live it down :p*

Northish: *@Wrenfair Try moaning it while awake in bed with @Izzily. I bet you'll get a different result.*

Izzily: *@Northish Please don't encourage @Wrenfair*

I chuckled at my brother's antics with his roommate and best friend, Wren. That Isidore teased Wren so much was a dead giveaway at how much he secretly liked him. I was about to say something to Felix when a comment further below caught my attention.

DannyDoMe69: *You really went on OUR Paris vacation without me? And now you're fucking around with another man like I meant nothing to you? Fuck you, Felix. I'm done trying to get you back. I hope you choke on his dick and die!*

Furious rage churned in my stomach that anyone would dare to speak like that to Felix, let alone a man who supposedly loved him once. I wanted to reach through the screen and pull his ex-boyfriend through it to exact a more fitting revenge for what he had put Felix through. Everything in me wished to tear his ex apart and set fire to his soul so he would burn in eternal damnation. I was not a violent person, but seeing Danny's comment filled me with a baffling level of anger. It begged to be unleashed on the bastard who dared to treat somebody as wonderful as Felix in such a manner.

Even more confusing was how his words made me long to wrap Felix up in my arms to protect him from anyone who wished to harm him. Why did it pain me that his loving heart had been wasted on such an undeserving cretin? It was a slight consolation that his ex's message did not hurt Felix, but that was upsetting in and of itself. That he was unaffected by such horrifying comments told me a lot of things about how Danny must have talked to him which sickened me. How could I have such a powerful, visceral reaction when I barely knew the kid?

"Are you okay?" His tone caused me to glance up,

only to see his worried expression. "You kinda look like you want to murder my phone."

I had to force myself to unclench my fingers from their tight grip on his mobile. "It is unacceptable! *Non*, it is unforgivable!"

"It is what it is. Now that I know he's pissed, blocking him is going to be even more gratifying. I should have done it ages ago, but I didn't want to give him the satisfaction of knowing he got to me. I don't give a shit now, though. He can go fuck a light socket for all I care. I'm done with his bullshit for good."

"He can never be allowed to speak to you like this again."

Felix tilted his head with a curious expression. "Wait, are you upset?"

"How could I not be by such a horrible message?" I remembered to return his mobile to him. "For him to speak to you that way after you offered him your heart makes him the worst kind of man."

My words seemed to please him. "If you want to shit-talk him, I'm here for it."

"That *boy* was not worthy of you," I told him. "You are far too good for the likes of one such as him. You deserve to be treasured by someone who will worship and adore you."

"Well, if you know of anyone who's interested in doing that, feel free to set me up with them. I've had absolute shit luck trying to find true love on my own."

For some strange reason, the thought of setting him up with somebody made jealousy surge within me, a feeling I had no right to experience. Once again, a powerful urge to hold him closer and never let him go overcame me. *Perhaps Isidore was right to warn me after all.*

Felix tapped his screen a few times before showing me he had blocked his ex-boyfriend's username. "Problem solved."

The vise clenched around my heart loosened, knowing that awful man would be unable to reach him anymore. "*Très bien.* I am glad you have bid *au revoir* to him for good."

His grin soothed my agitated soul like a calming balm. "Same. Do you know what the best part is?"

"What?"

His smile turned wicked and stirred my lust. "Now you have a chance to kiss me without it being for revenge."

A disturbingly large part of me wanted to pull him across the table and claim his lips as mine. But I restrained myself to a smirk. "I shall keep it in mind. Come, let us continue with our day."

His joyful reaction did things to my heart I could not explain. For some reason, it seemed to be of the utmost importance to make him laugh and forget all about his horrible ex-boyfriend. I was more determined than before to ensure Felix enjoyed himself to the fullest in Paris.

Chapter 3

Felix

"Thanks for walking me to my hotel. I would have gotten lost on my own."

Arsène looked up at the sky with a beautiful smile. "It is a lovely night for a walk, *non?*"

He may have been searching for the stars, but I couldn't stop looking at his handsome face. Even in profile, he was stunningly gorgeous. It was like being on an evening stroll with Prince Charming. "It sure is. Everything has been perfect today."

"I am glad you are enjoying your stay here."

That was an understatement. "Only because you've been an amazing tour guide. This beats the hell out of being lost and frustrated."

His chuckle sent shivers quaking through me. "That is encouraging to hear."

"So, speaking of things that have nothing to do with that: when do I get to hold up my end of our bargain? I feel bad I've taken so many selfies of us together, but you haven't taken any of me." Well, I said I felt bad, but I was still over the moon I had so much evidence of the best day and kisses of my life. A better person might have felt guilty, but fuck that shit.

"We will have plenty of time for that later. Today, I wanted you to focus on enjoying this beautiful city."

It was a touching show of consideration. "Thanks for that. Does that mean your studio is part of the tour? Because I'd really like to see it."

"Oh?"

I tried to think of a reason that didn't sound creepy to justify my interest. "Well, you *said* it was famous. It seems like it should be on the itinerary."

"*Oui*, I did say that." He grinned, making me fucking swoon again. Damn it, nobody should be *that* attractive! "That can be arranged."

Excitement bubbled up inside me, but I tried to keep my cool. "Great, I'd love to see where the magic happens."

"I was unaware that my bedroom was on your list of landmarks to visit." His devilish smirk set my lust aflame, causing me to stumble. I flushed when he reached out to steady me, his hand lingering on me longer than was strictly necessary, sending my heart racing.

My horniness got the better of me. "Well, my goal is to see all that Paris has to offer."

His voice was a sensual purr as he leaned closer to ask, "And what are you hoping my bedroom will offer you?"

"A good time?"

"Ah, but I can offer you a good time anywhere."

I flashed a cheeky grin, thriving off the banter. "Promise?"

"We shall see." He gave me a flirty wink that sent my

hormones into a tizzy. Was it really so wrong I wanted to bang him like a pinky toe against a coffee table?

He doused my eagerness when he pointed out, "There is your hotel."

Augie had flipped out when he found out I was planning to slum it in a youth hostel. His solution was to book me a stay at the expensive Luxurian Hotel Suites that was so far out of my price range it wasn't even funny. As incredible as the hotel was, it was the last place I wanted to be at the moment, because that meant leaving Arsène for the night.

I couldn't keep the disappointment out of my voice. "Great."

To my surprise, he pressed me against the wall by the hotel door, pinning me with his arm braced behind me. It was an epic test of willpower for me not to get hard over how badly I wanted him to ravish me. That became significantly more difficult when he leaned in to murmur in a sensuous rumble, *"Bonne nuit,* Monsieur Felix." I sank further back to hide my burgeoning erection he inspired by speaking French so close to me in such a suggestive position. "Shall I kiss you goodbye the French way?"

"Do you mean on each cheek or with tongue? Because I know which one I'm voting for."

He chuckled before he pressed a gentle kiss on each of my cheeks, then said something in French that sounded sexy as fuck.

He smirked as I stared up at him with wide eyes. I clenched my hands into fists at my side to stop myself from grabbing his shirt to yank him down again into a desperate kiss with tongue. "What does that mean?"

Arsène used his free hand to trace the outline of my jaw as his gaze dropped to my lips. I held my breath as everything in me silently begged, *Fucking fuck me!*

The sexy bastard had the audacity to answer my question instead of making out with me. "I wished you pleasant dreams." He lowered his voice, turning me into a quivering puddle. "Perhaps I shall visit you in them tonight to ensure you do."

The words were out of my mouth before I could talk myself out of them. "Or you could just stay."

He rubbed his thumb over my lower lip. "If I did, you would not get any sleep, let alone have sweet dreams."

"That sounds like a tradeoff I'm willing to make."

The corner of his lips turned up in a smile. "Perhaps another night. Tonight, you must rest. It has been a very long day."

"Is that your way of telling me to keep up my strength because I'm going to need it?"

I loved the sound of his laughter, and how it made the light dance in his golden eyes. "Keep thinking good thoughts, *chéri*." Oh, I *really* enjoyed being called that. "I will see you in the morning."

"And in my dreams?"

"*Oui, fais de beaux rêves.*" He placed a tender kiss on my forehead that melted my heart. "Yes, make beautiful dreams tonight, and we will have even more adventures tomorrow."

How was I supposed to form words after *that*? It was

only with a heroic effort that I got out, "I'm looking forward to both."

With a final caress, Arsène patted my cheek, then stepped away with a smile. "As am I. *Au revoir*, Monsieur Felix."

Him speaking French equaled an instant erection. Great, that wouldn't be inconvenient at *all*. I peeled myself off the wall and slinked inside, praying he didn't notice I was hard as a diamond.

Safe in my luxurious hotel room, I warred with myself over jerking off or being a good baby brother and calling Augie like I promised. I wanted to rub one out, but I wasn't in the mood to rush it. After that kind of teasing, it deserved a proper fantasy to get off to—which meant waiting until I finished assuaging my older brother's anxieties.

Despite the nine-hour time difference, he logged on so we could video chat. His brow furrowed with worry as he assessed me. "Are you okay?"

"Hello to you, too."

His answering scowl killed my erection at record speed.

Brody joined Augie on the couch, saying with his beautiful Irish brogue, "Be nice to your brother."

I pretended to play dumb. "Are you telling me or him?"

"You. Augie has been worried about you since before you left." He wrapped an arm around his boyfriend's shoulder in a loose hug. "I keep trying to distract him, but—"

It was too tempting to not joke about. "Ohhh, so *that's* why he has a hickey on his neck."

My brother looked dour as he muttered, "I don't have a hickey."

"We can change that later," Brody teased him, brushing his thumb against Augie's neck.

Augie shivered as he glared at his boyfriend. "There will be no hickeys, thank you very much." He returned his attention to me. "Please tell me you're okay. Are you okay? I need you to be okay."

Because our mom had died when we were young, Augie took his responsibility as an older brother seriously. He always fretted about me, which in his defense, I had given him plenty to worry about over the years. I quit being such a jerk to him. "I'm better than okay. This hotel is incredible, and today was the best day I've had in a really long time. Arsène has taken very good care of me."

"Based on that kiss, I'd say so," Brody joked.

It shocked me when my brother asked, "Kiss? What kiss?"

Brody at least had the decency to look sheepish. "Sorry, I thought you had caved and checked his social media."

"You told me all he had posted was the Eiffel Tower and lunch!"

"That wasn't technically a lie. The Eiffel Tower was in the picture. And video."

"*Video?*" I winced as Augie made an outraged noise as he pulled out his phone to watch the clip I had shared. "What the fuck is this? Felix!"

I had hoped that by posting everything earlier that my brother would have had already gotten over his initial reaction. It stunned me he had waited so long to check my social media; I figured he would have been obsessively refreshing it all day. I attributed it to Brody's successful attempts at distracting him with sex. "Relax, it wasn't a real kiss."

"Bullshit!"

Brody took a more joking approach. "That doesn't seem to have stopped you from enjoying it."

I glared at him when his comment upset Augie further. "You can stop helping now."

He flashed a roguish grin that made me roll my eyes. "You need all the help you can get, lad."

Augie raised his voice as he demanded, "What do you mean that wasn't real? It sure as hell looked real to me. What were you thinking?"

As always, Brody had a smart-ass answer. "Probably 'Take me now,' I'd imagine." Well, he wasn't wrong about that.

I groaned in frustration as my brother rewatched the video for a third time. "Look, it's not what you think. I know it's petty, but I wanted to piss off Danny that someone so hot was interested in me. Arsène played along. We staged it."

Augie continued flipping through the other pictures I had posted of me and Arsène cuddling with sweet kisses. "I don't believe you. Nobody is that good of an actor!"

"Oh, please. We all know I'm not cute enough to land somebody like him for real." I scoffed at the ridiculous notion. "He's too hot, too famous, and too old to be interested in a kid like me. He's just humoring me."

"There's nothing wrong with having a little fun," Brody assured me. "Especially when it's with someone as gorgeous as that."

Augie hid his face in his hand and groaned. "Please don't encourage him to break his own damn heart. Men who look like him leave a trail of shattered dreams in their wake."

"I'll be fine," I reassured him. "It was just for show. I'm under no illusions it was anything more than that."

"It won't be with that attitude."

Augie huffed. "Brody, stop encouraging him."

"He's young, he's cute, and it looks like he's in good hands," he replied with a shrug. "He should enjoy his holiday to the fullest."

"Thank you, Brody. I appreciate the support." He always came through for me. "Seriously, I'm fine. Paris is amazing, the food is incredible, and everything is wonderful. I know it's pointless to tell you to stop worrying so much, but stop worrying so much."

Augie took a deep breath to calm himself. "I'm glad you're enjoying yourself. For the sake of my mental well-being, please stay safe."

I squashed my urge to crack a joke about getting into danger. "Arsène won't let anything bad happen to me. You have my word that I'll be on my best behavior."

"It's been a long day. Maybe the thing that would help Felix the most is getting a good night's sleep. We should let him go." I mentally hugged Brody for his suggestion.

Augie sighed. "You're right. Promise you'll call me tomorrow night?"

"I promise. We're going to the Louvre in the morning, so it'll be another entertaining day."

"See? Nice and educational." Brody ruffled my older brother's hair. "You have nothing to worry about. Do you need another distraction?"

Augie's cheeks turned pink at the innuendo. "Love you, Felix. Stay safe."

"Love you both, too. I'll message you in the morning so you know the boogeyman didn't kidnap me overnight."

After a few more words, we ended the call. I loved my brother, but sometimes his worrying was a bit much.

I checked my notifications and grinned when I saw I had received several texts from North about the images of Arsène I had shared. He was an awesome roommate and friend, who could get down in the gutter with the best of them. Having a sweetheart for a boyfriend hadn't reformed his dirty mind any. He was so cute with Elias and they were perfect for each other. I hadn't spent much time hanging out with his new boyfriend, but I already liked him a lot. Their relationship gave me hope that if someone who didn't believe in love like North had found it, there was still a chance for me.

Since he was around, we got on a video call. As per usual, North wore jeans and a green T-shirt. His boy-next-door good looks made his career as a romance novelist twice as funny to me, especially when his books were so explicit. I could tell from his broad grin how amused he was by what I had posted on social media. "Dude, I'm *so* proud of you. You haven't even been in Paris a full day yet, and you're already hooking up with hot guys! Good for you, Felix."

"I figured it'd impress you, even if it was only one guy and not multiple."

He laughed. "I'm more than impressed! He's combust-your-clothes-off levels of sexiness. How did you meet Mr. Handsome?"

"He's actually Izzy's older brother, Arsène, who is playing tour guide for me."

North's jaw dropped. "Are you shitting me? He doesn't look anything like the picture Izzy showed us."

"Yeah, the scruff really changes his appearance." It was hard not to grow distracted by the thought.

"I'd say." His lips curved up into an impish smirk. "Did you draw the line at kissing, or were you a bold adventurer on a sexual conquest?"

Making myself more comfortable in the desk chair, I tried not to sound as disappointed as I felt. "It was a staged kiss to piss off my ex-boyfriend. The wildest part of the story is he agreed to do it before I realized who he was."

North's eyebrows arched up at that tidbit. "Wait, so you asked to make out with someone you thought was a total stranger?"

"In my defense, I assumed it would be a cute peck on the cheek, not toe-curling bliss."

"Now, *that's* what I'm talking about!" North fist-pumped the air. "He's obviously down to fuck, so go for it!"

I refused to believe it. "Kissing me as a joke doesn't mean he wants to sleep with me."

"Bullshit. Based on that video, he's *more* than into the idea."

"Sure, we flirted a bit when he dropped me off at the hotel, but I think he's just having fun teasing me." The thought filled me with an uncomfortable heat as I shifted in my chair. "Even if he was interested, I'm leaving in a few days. There's no point."

"What do you mean? Fun is *always* worth it."

I knew he spoke from personal experience, but I had lived a much different life. "Yeah, but he's Izzy's older brother. I'm pretty sure hooking up with him is breaking some friendship rule." That hadn't stopped me from flirting back, but in a calmer moment, it gave me reason to pause.

"And kissing him doesn't?"

Damn it, he had me there. "Maybe if it was real. It was just a joke, plus I cleared it with Izzy before I posted everything. Don't forget, he specifically cautioned me not to fall for his brother."

"If you're only looking for sexy fun times and nothing more, heartbreak won't be an issue. Your dick doesn't have a heart to break."

I snickered at that. "Wow, that's a line you should use in one of your books."

"Yeah, you're right. I should write that down before I forget." He took out his phone and jotted down the quote for later. "I say you do you and don't worry about Izzy. Enjoy having fun with Arsène. You deserve it after what your shithead ex put you through. This is your perfect chance to indulge in the best sex of your life with no strings attached."

"The problem with that is I have a terrible habit of attaching strings when I shouldn't." I sighed in frustration at myself. Why was keeping my heart out of romance so hard? Life would be so much easier if I wasn't a hopeless romantic. "But then again, this is different. There's an ocean separating us once I go home, so it's not like I have any hope for anything more than a casual fling."

North continued encouraging me. "Exactly! This is a fantastic chance to live a little and get your rocks off at the same time. If nothing else, it would be great research for your writing."

It was a fair point. I had always dabbled with writing in secret, but he found out after discovering a forgotten notebook in our living room. After that, he had relentlessly encouraged me to embrace writing and the romance genre. It had always embarrassed me I liked romance since I was a guy. The last thing I expected was finding out North was a romance novelist named Finch Northish. His success gave me the courage to pursue it, but I still didn't think I was any good. North vehemently disagreed, though. When he was allergic to bullshit and knew what he was talking about since he was a published author, I almost had no choice but to believe him.

Still, it was hard to write about romance when my dating life had been so lacking in that department.

Combined with having no experience with casual sex, I felt there were too many believability gaps in my work. "I don't know. It would be creepy if I hooked up with him, then wrote a book about a guy who falls in love with an older tour guide."

"The only person who would know it's based on anything real is you."

"And you, and all of our other friends if they read it. I couldn't look Izzy in the eyes again if he knew I wrote a book about banging his older brother like a screen door in a hurricane."

North cracked up at my description. "Write that down for your future book. I wouldn't worry about Izzy, though. We all know he's too cool and above it all to get bothered about it."

He was right about that. Izzy had a chill, aloof air that I envied. Nothing ever seemed to bother him; he was completely unflappable, which was a miracle when he was friends with the rest of our zany group. "True, but *I* would be uncomfortable around him knowing I based it on my sexual misadventures with Arsène, even if he didn't give a shit."

"Nobody is saying you should write a veiled autobiography about your sexual adventures together," North reasoned with me. "But it's a fantastic opportunity to enjoy an inspirational deep-dicking with one of the hottest guys ever. You'd be a fool not to take him up on his offer."

I snorted at the ridiculous idea. "Excuse me while I

laugh for an eternity about his dick being a quill and dipping into my asshole inkwell to write a sexy romance."

North howled with laughter. "See? He's already inspiring your imagination."

"I'm pretty sure that's just me being me."

He finally regained his composure. "Look, you've always worried about not having enough experiences dating to make your writing realistic. This is a great opportunity to research the hit-it-and-quit-it lifestyle. You couldn't ask for a better invitation than someone that gorgeous ready to give you the fuck of a lifetime."

"I'll see what tomorrow brings." I shrugged, still not convinced Arsène would be into me, despite all his teasing. "How are things with you and Elias?"

I couldn't help but envy his blissful expression. "He continues to be the best thing that's ever happened to me. He should be here any minute."

"Please remember to sanitize everything after you're done being amorous on every flat surface outside your bedroom." I was only half-joking; there was no doubt in my mind that the couple would take advantage of the empty apartment.

North chuckled. "Are you implying we're going to be swinging from the chandeliers with wild sex since you're not here?"

"Save the chandelier sex for your mom's house. She actually has them." North's mom, Linda, was a big fan of shiny and had five of them in her house—including in her closet.

"Hold on, I think he's here." North got up to answer the door.

His twin sister, West, came bounding over and plopped herself in front of the computer with an excited squeal. She wore a navy-and-white overbust corset that looked like the TARDIS from *Doctor Who*. It was paired with white pants, and her always dazzling glitter eye shadow and ruby-red lips. "Oh my god, Fifi!" She was the only person who could call me that and live. Because of her brother, she hung out all the time at our apartment and had become one of my closest friends. She was like a sister to me, with the bonus of not being a worrywart like my own sibling. "I *can't* with those pictures you posted earlier! And that video? Holy shit! So. Fucking. Hot! I'm so proud of you, babe! Please tell me you didn't stop there."

"Sorry to disappoint you, Westie, but it was nothing but blue balls and flirting off camera."

She shrugged. "Well, it's only been a day. I trust you intrigued him enough to want to pounce on you the first chance he gets tomorrow."

"From your lips to his ears."

"More like from his lips to your dick, am I right?"

It was impossible not to laugh at that. "Something like that. Speaking of which, since North hasn't returned yet, I'm assuming he's making out with Elias?"

"He sure is." West catcalled her brother beyond the laptop monitor. "Come on, you can do better than that! Use your tongue!"

I heard North yell at her, "The only thing stopping me is you!"

"Tough shit! I'm not leaving when Fifi is here!"

He came over and shoved his twin over on the couch. "God forbid I get between you and your precious Fifi."

West blew me a kiss I pretended to catch and press to my cheek. "I'd take him and Elias over you any day of the week."

When Elias tried to sit down, his boyfriend pulled him onto his lap into a hug. He was cute as hell in that shy, nerdy kind of way with his rimless glasses, soft features, and lavender polo paired with faded jeans. "Hi, Felix! How's Paris?"

"Amazing! There's so much to do here."

I rolled my eyes when North and West snickered at my choice of words. "Really, you two?"

"Hey, you said it, not me," North said with a shrug.

Elias was kind enough to distract us from his boyfriend's dirty mind. "Paris is such a wonderful city. I've been there several times with Mom on vacation."

"We're going to the Louvre tomorrow. I don't know much about art, but I'm excited."

"Even if you're not into art, it's still a great place to visit. Everyone always wants to see the *Mona Lisa*, but definitely check out the *Winged Victory of Samothrace* statue. Since it's one of their most famous sculptures, Arsène should have no problem finding it for you."

"Do you have any other recommendations for things to do while I'm here? I didn't have a chance to ask you before I left."

Elias tapped his chin while he considered my question. "Try a true French croissant, but as a warning, they *will* ruin American ones for you. It's worth it, though. Oh, and you can't go wrong with pastries of any kind."

"I second both recommendations," West added. "Check out my list I sent you of my favorite places I discovered during my summer abroad last year."

North hugged his boyfriend closer. "We should do a couples' vacation sometime."

Elias's radiant smile was so adorable. North had lucked out with such a cute boyfriend. I tried not to feel a pang of envy. "That would be wonderful. I'd love to return to Italy. Between the delicious food and the amazing museums, there's so many reasons to visit."

"All the pasta and gelato I can eat? Count me in!"

"Fine, you two can go be lovebirds together, while Fifi and I live it up with his gorgeous new boy toy."

I had to laugh. "I don't think you can call someone as manly as Arsène a 'boy toy.'"

"That depends on how you use him. If you need some tips, I've got a few tricks you can use to blow his mind."

"Don't you mean blow his dick?" North asked with a snort.

"Considering most guys with dicks think with their tiny heads, I stand by my original statement," West retorted with a smirk. "It's basically the same thing."

As enjoyable as talking to my friends was, I stifled a yawn. "Thanks for chatting with me, but I'm going to hit the shower and crash. Jet lag is kicking my ass."

West gave me a playful look. "That sounds like code for 'I need to go jerk off now.'"

"Great, it sounds like you should go, too," North told her. "Elias and I have some catching up to do."

She blew a raspberry at him. "You're no fun. Elias, make him be nice to me."

"Yes, please make me be nice to her." North started kissing his way up his boyfriend's neck, making him shiver. "West, it's time for you to leave."

She sighed dramatically. "Fine, be a brat. Fifi, we'll catch up soon, okay?"

"I'll text you tomorrow."

"With juicy details about your hookup with Monsieur Sexy?"

I snorted at that. "It's an art museum, Westie. That's not the place to find inspiration to get down and dirty."

"With your imagination, I'm sure you can come up with some amorous ideas from all those paintings and sculptures of naked men."

I rolled my eyes. "If you say so."

"Enjoy yourself to the fullest tomorrow. Do anything I used to do. You'll thank me for it later." North winked at me for good measure.

I laughed again. "Sadly, I don't have the balls to say to his face, 'You're so hot, we *have* to fuck.' Only you could pull that kind of shit off. I've never been that smooth, ever."

"Hey, it works better than you'd think. The worst he could do is say no, right?"

"No, he could get offended and refuse to play tour

guide for me, which would be significantly worse. Not to mention my ego wouldn't survive the rejection."

"Trust me, he won't say no."

West ran her fingers through her platinum-white hair with rainbow ombre highlights. "You know how much I hate agreeing with North, but he's right. Any guy who makes out with you like that is down to fuck you into being fluent in French."

"Damn, no wonder I was hopeless learning it in high school. I wasn't making out with the right guys," I said with a laugh. "It was nice catching up with all of you. I'll be in touch tomorrow."

We exchanged a few more parting words before I ended the call. Resisting the urge to collapse in bed, I went to the bathroom for a quick shower. At least, that was my original intention. But left alone with my thoughts, memories of the hottest kiss of my life replayed, making me rock-hard once more. I gave myself over to the full fantasy of what could have been if Arsène had stayed.

The spark of interest in his eyes set fire to my soul. Still pressed against the wall, I embedded my fingers in his hair as we kissed. I loved the way he dominated me. It was incredible enjoying myself with a man who knew what to do with me. He further proved that when he cupped his hand around my arousal. He smirked against my lips when I rocked into his touch, desperate for relief.

"So eager," he teased me, still toying with me over my clothes.

"Eager and willing, so stop playing with me."

Growling in frustration, I refused to give myself blue balls in my own damn fantasy. There was plenty of time to enjoy a prolonged, realistic daydream later. It was time to speed things up to the exciting part.

I braced myself against the hotel window as Arsène entered me from behind. The view of the Eiffel Tower was great, but not nearly as amazing as the feeling of him possessively gripping my hips. I pushed against him with a groan, needing more.

He obliged me by tugging on the shell of my ear with his teeth, then murmured something in French that made me weak in the knees. I tried to touch myself, but he denied me. Before I could complain, he reached around to stroke my cock. I thrust into his fist as he worked me, everything blurring into a pleasurable haze.

He hummed with interest. "How unexpected."

"What is?"

"I expected you to be louder."

The comment caused me to bristle. "Why? Because I'm American?"

"No, because you're chatty, and we're alone in your mind."

Wow, nothing like getting called out in your own fantasy. Sadly, it wasn't the first time, nor the last. Something told me I wasn't too far off base with how the real Arsène would react. The shittiest part was he was right; I rarely shut up unless I was sucking a dick or asleep.

"Fine, fuck me harder! Is that better?"

His answer came in the form of him pulling out and spinning me around to slam my back hard against the window. Gasping at the sudden shock of the cold glass pane, I didn't resist as he lifted me up to wrap my legs around him. As he started pounding into me, I shouted as I clung to him while he fucked me like I had never been fucked before. I held nothing back as I called out to him, riding him for everything he was worth.

He claimed my lips in a savage kiss. I could only whimper as my toes curled from the overload of pleasure. "Arsène, please!"

"And what are you begging for so beautifully?"

"I'm so close! Let me come."

His mischievous smile was too much when combined with him purring, "As you wish, chéri."

The nickname alone was enough to trigger my orgasm in my mind and reality. I staggered against the tile wall from the intensity of my release, dazed from the experience. It took me a moment to return to myself. And because I was a total weirdo, I felt guilty that I came when fake Arsène didn't. I washed off my hand as I returned to my fantasy.

"I thought I lost you," he said with sexy smugness.

"You did, but I'm back now."

His hips kept driving into me. "How considerate of you to return so I can finish."

"I'm nothing if not thoughtful." He snorted at my claim, so I shoved his shoulder. "Hey, don't laugh! I refuse to be mocked by my own imagination."

He continued teasing me. "You are so cute when you pout."

"I—"

Arsène cut my next protest off with a kiss. My irritation melted as I lost myself in his considerable skill. He pushed in deep as he came, moaning my name.

We rested our foreheads against each other as we basked in the afterglow. He then treated me to a sweet kiss I savored while still hugging him. "I cannot wait to do this with you for real, chéri."

"Wow, I didn't know I was that much of an optimist and a glutton for punishment."

"You would enjoy my punishment."

Rolling my eyes, I told him, "I doubt it. You seem like you'd be the kind of bastard who would be super into edging me until I was ready to break."

"It is one of the many ways I have to make you beg for more."

"Ha, I wouldn't give you the satisfaction of that."

His smug smirk was hot as hell. "That is big talk for someone who fantasized about sweeping all the dishes off the table at the restaurant and having me fuck him in front of everyone."

"Oh, please. Like you wouldn't have enjoyed getting arrested for that."

"I would not have stopped until we both came. If you wish for me to use handcuffs on you—"

"Nope, I'm pruning in the shower and exhausted, so we're not going down that road tonight. Save it for tomorrow night when I come home sexually frustrated after another day of enduring your sexiness."

Leave it to me to be ridiculed by a figment of my

imagination. Being a writer had some really weird aspects to it sometimes.

Satisfied that I hadn't left the dream Arsène in the lurch, I got out of the shower. It was a relief to collapse into bed. I sank into the soft sheets and mattress with a happy sigh. Bless my brother's anxieties for insisting I had a better room than I'd ever be able to afford on my own.

I had barely pictured Arsène curling up behind me to spoon before I fell asleep with a smile on my face.

Chapter 4

Arsène

AFTER SPENDING SIX HOURS walking the halls of the Louvre, I expected Felix to be tired, fidgety, and more than ready to go somewhere else filled with less history. I did not think I would be the one requesting we take a break on a bench to rest for a few minutes.

He sighed happily as he looked at the paintings hanging around us in the gallery. "It almost seems like an insult to call this place incredible, because it's so beyond amazing!"

"Is it everything you hoped it would be?"

"That and more!" His boundless enthusiasm was adorable. It was refreshing being with someone so vivacious, who enjoyed himself to the fullest. "Thank you for bringing me here. It wouldn't have been nearly as fun wandering around and reading the plaques by myself."

"There are always the audio guides."

He scoffed. "Unless they also tell funny dick jokes about naked Greek statues from the BC era like you do, I'm not interested. You make it about more than just some carved stone or paint on a canvas."

"That is kind of you to say."

Felix grinned at me with a boyish charm that was far

more beautiful to me than the priceless art surrounding us. "It's also true. How do you know so much about art?"

"I attended a few art history classes while I was studying at university in New York." It felt like a lifetime ago, but I still remembered a lot of what I learned because it had fascinated me. "I thought it would help my photography."

"Did you always want to be a photographer?"

I nodded. "Since I was a boy."

"You're so lucky you've always known what you wanted to do with your life. I hate not knowing what I'm doing in the future. My brother wouldn't have to worry so much if I could figure out my shit."

"What are you studying at university?"

Rubbing the back of his head, he looked almost sheepish. "You promise you won't laugh?"

"You have my word."

"My major is folklore." He looked at me as if he expected me to go against my word and mock him. When I did not, he continued. "I was undecided for a while, but when I found out about gay fairytales, I decided I wanted to study that."

I raised my eyebrows in surprise. "There are gay fairytales?"

"It's a little-known fact that there were quite a lot of LGBTQ+ ones way back when." Felix grew more excited when he realized he had a captive audience. "But when fairytales moved from being an oral tradition to a written one around the 1850s and 1900s, a bunch of fucking prudes edited them into something more 'acceptable' to their social standards. Stith Thompson was almost single-handedly responsible for eliminating the LGBTQ+ canon of fairy tales. But a few got through his censorship, so I study that."

"How remarkable. I had no idea there were any."

"I know it's weird for a guy to be into romantic happily ever afters, but I've always been drawn to them." He made a face. "It's super fascinating to study, but folklore isn't a practical subject like business or something in STEM. I don't have a clue what I'm going to do with that degree when I graduate."

"What is your passion?"

He ruffled his hair, making it stand up in little spikes. "I enjoy writing, but I'm nowhere close to being good enough to sustain myself doing it. Romance is a super-competitive genre, and it's tough trying to make a name for yourself when you're nobody. Of course, it's extra hard to do that when I haven't finished a single book yet."

I did not miss the insecurity that came with being as young as Felix. "You do not have to be the best to be successful. There are lots of terrible writers making millions."

Instead of comforting him as I had hoped, he curled up on himself with a groan. "Gee, thanks. That makes me feel even worse knowing no matter how good I am, I'll never make that kind of money doing what I love."

"Do you think any of them imagined the careers they have now before they published their first book?"

He shrugged. "Probably not."

"Success is a funny thing. It finds you when you least expect it."

Felix looked at me with his gorgeous jade-colored eyes. They moved something inside me I had almost forgotten existed—my heart. "What about you?"

Lost in his green gaze, I didn't understand what he meant. "What about me?"

"Did you ever imagine you'd have the world-famous, successful career that you have now?"

"My arrogant ego never had any doubts." His crestfallen expression hurt, and I hurried to make it go away. "But my fear was a different story."

"How so?"

It was something I had never talked about before, but for some strange reason, I felt I owed Felix honesty. "I was afraid that the world would have a negative opinion of my talent. Even now, with all the fame and money my success has brought me, there is a tiny part of my heart that fears the day it all disappears when someone new and more exciting takes my place. But I put myself out there, because it is in my marrow to do what I do. I cannot be anyone other than me."

I did not blame him for seeming surprised. "Do you actually suffer from imposter syndrome, or are you only saying that to make me feel better?"

"You are the only person I have ever told that truth." I covered his hand with mine to give it a squeeze. "The hardest lesson I had to learn was that if I did not love my own work, I could not expect anyone else to do so. In order to move forward, you should always be your own biggest fan."

It pleased me when he did not pull away from my touch. "I'm my own worst critic, though. I think everything I write is shit."

"You must learn to be kind to yourself, then. It is one thing to have a critical eye, but it is bad when you use that to hurt yourself." I hoped he would take my words to heart. "Tell me something positive about your writing."

He remained silent as he attempted to come up with a compliment. "Um, I know how to use commas?"

I shook my head. "*Non*, you can do much better than that. That is like saying, 'I am skilled at ending a sentence with a period.' Try again."

"Hey, in my defense, most people can't properly use a comma to save their life." He scowled when I gave him a look that told him I refused to accept such nonsense. "Fine. The best thing I have going for my writing is I have a *very* vivid imagination."

He piqued my interest with that comment. "That is good for writing and many other things. Some more perverse than others."

Felix sat up straighter. "What adventures I get up to in the privacy of my mind is my business alone."

I leaned closer to murmur in his ear, "Unless you want help turning your dreams into reality."

He shied away from me, but he was far from embarrassed. "Are you volunteering?"

"To make your dreams come true?" The endless possibilities pleased me. "You could persuade me."

The thrill in his eyes sent heat flaring through me. I was getting into dangerous territories, but I could not stop myself from barreling full speed ahead. "And how could I do that?"

Considering my interest in him, all he would have to say was "Please." But I pretended to put up some resistance as a test. "Telling me what your fantasy is would be a good place to start, *non*?"

"What makes you assume it's a fantasy and not a regular dream?"

I reached over and caressed his flushed cheek. "Your beautiful blush."

A cute squeak escaped from him, but I admired he didn't back down. "Maybe I'm just hot."

"You are *very* hot."

His laughter filled my soul with sunshine. "If you say so, Monsieur Sexy." He rolled his eyes with an indignant scoff. "Please, I'm a string bean next to you. You've got to be joking."

"If that were true, I would be thinking very different thoughts."

His spark of curiosity returned. "What kind of thoughts *are* you thinking now?"

I licked my lips as I resisted the urge to claim his. "Ones that will get us into trouble."

"Because we're in public?" His smile turned wicked, which caused my cock to stir with interest. "Is public indecency illegal here, too?"

I had to laugh at his eagerness. "Indeed, it is."

"So, what you're telling me is we need a change in

location to enjoy being indecent with each other? Because that's what I'm hearing."

"You are too tempting, *chéri*. You make me want to do things my brother would not approve of."

"Then it's a good thing he's not here, because I'm in the mood to get in some sexy trouble." It took serious restraint not to take him on the bench when he added, "I guess the real question is, do you want to make my dreams come true? Because all of them involve you and me naked."

It broke the small shred of willpower I had. I leaned over and kissed him hard, uncaring of who was watching. I burned with an unfamiliar need to claim him, to make him mine.

He was breathless when we parted. "I'll take that as a yes?"

"*Oui*."

I brought Felix to my apartment above my studio. I ached to capture the moment with my camera, but I wanted him too much. The gentleman in me needed him to be sure, though. "Is this what you want?"

"You inside me? Absofuckinglutely." He reached out and tugged on my shirt to draw me flush against him. "I want you to show me that good time you promised me last night, because I'm dying for a satisfying fuck after a long dry spell."

Remembering my younger brother's warning, I had to ask, "Do you not fear falling in love with me?"

"I'm more afraid of going home and regretting not taking a chance on enjoying the best sex of my life." His pleading gaze once again made me experience an unexpected surge of emotions. "I know it's pure fantasy that somebody as gorgeous, talented, and famous as you would ever be interested in someone as scrawny and young as me. But if you want me, I want to live this dream for as long as I can."

I cupped his face in my hands as I told him with the utmost sincerity, "I want you, *chéri*. You are a cute and charming smart-ass, which is an irresistible combination. It would be a shame to waste another night regretting being a gentleman and leaving you alone in bed without me to keep you company."

His eyes went wide in surprise. "You're not just saying that, are you? You honestly mean it."

"More than I ever thought possible." I bent down to kiss him, teasing at first, then going deeper. His surrender was intoxicating. I could not get enough of his tongue dancing against mine. It took effort to pull back and remove his shirt. It was true he did not have the defined, muscular body of the models I worked with, but he was no less beautiful because of it. He was pale and lithe, but very much a man.

Felix returned the favor by stripping me of my shirt, lighting up at the sight of my toned physique. He ran his fingers down my chest and over my defined abs. "God, when you look like this, why did you decide to have a career behind the camera instead of in front of it?"

"I am not very good at taking directions." It was heavenly to follow the curve of his spine with my fingertips. "My preference in most things is to be the one in control."

There was no hesitation as he reached for the button of my pants and unzipped them. "You want to dominate me?"

"Dominate your desires," I clarified as I helped him out of his jeans. It freed me up to slide mine off and kick aside. "I will not be satisfied until my name is the only word you remember."

He inhaled sharply when I fondled him over his bright purple briefs. "Promise?"

"*Oui.*" I slid off his underwear, enjoying the show when his arousal sprung free to stand at full attention. I groped his firm ass before giving in to the temptation to stroke his rigid length. "*C'est magnifique.*" I smirked when his member twitched in my hand. "Which pleased you more: the compliment or the French?"

"Both. Definitely both." He slid off my black briefs with a leer. My ego purred at his reaction to my erection. "You magnificent bastard."

"I am glad I meet with your approval." He teased me by wrapping his hand around me and stroking my hardness. "Shall we move this to the bed?"

"Please." He got in bed, stretching out on his back.

I enjoyed pinning him down, brushing our erections together. Stealing another taste of his lips, I trailed lingering kisses down his neck. He drew a shuddering breath as he trembled under me. His responsiveness was a huge turn-on, driving me to step things up. I toyed with his nipple until it tightened into a peak. It resulted in a delectable keen for my efforts. "Yes, let me hear you." To my surprise, he burst into laughter. "What is so funny?"

He did not give me a direct answer to my question. "Not to weird you out, but I needed some relief after you dropped me off yesterday."

"Did you touch yourself while thinking about what would have happened if I had gone up to your hotel room instead of home?" The thought of him doing so drew a groan of need from me.

He grinned at my reaction. "Oh, please tell me you did the same thing last night."

I was not ashamed to admit the truth. "It seems we are more similar than I previously believed."

"Fuck, that's so sexy," he whimpered. "In my fantasy, you complained I was too quiet as you pleasured me. I asked if you thought I'd be loud because I'm American, but you said no, it was because we were alone in my mind."

I laughed hard at his description. "Are you telling me you pleasured yourself to thoughts of us bickering?"

He was completely unrepentant. "What can I say? Banter gets me going."

"Oh, then we shall get along nicely. I am impressed you already know me well enough to understand I thrive on that and wish to hear your voice calling out to me." I tugged on his nipple with my teeth, which resulted in a very pleasing gasp. "*Oui*, just like that, *chéri*."

His giggle made my heart thud in my chest at how precious he was. "I can't believe I was right."

"What else did I say?"

"You said some things in French, but since I'm not fluent, I'm sure it was just sexy gibberish."

I chuckled as I continued down his thin trail of hair that led me closer to temptation. "Sexy gibberish? Is there such a thing?" I brushed my scuff against his inner thigh as I repositioned myself lower. It earned me a delicious whimper as I kissed my way to my goal.

"It had the desired effect, whatever it was."

"And what was that?"

His challenging gaze lit a fire inside me. "Me begging for more."

"I like the sound of that." Unable to resist anymore, I sucked one of his balls into my mouth to toy with it. His hands scrambled for a hold in the sheets as I lavished it with attention. His breathing became shaky, and I wondered what it would take to make him plead for more.

It turned out a swirl of my tongue combined with some suction was all that was necessary. "Arsène, please stop torturing me."

"But it is so much fun for me." I switched to the opposite one I had neglected, resulting in an adorably grumpy grumble. "Does this leave you unsatisfied?"

"Not to sound like a demanding dick, but yeah, it does."

I laughed at his forthright answer. "We cannot have that now, can we?" I did not wait for him to reply before I went down on him with great enthusiasm.

One of his hands found purchase in my hair as he held on to keep himself grounded. I loved hearing swears falling from his beautiful lips when I swallowed around his length. Relaxing my jaw, I took him in to the base. It did not surprise me when he came with a shout. I drank his release before drawing back, wiping the corner of my mouth as I looked down at him with burning need. "Do you wish to stop there?"

"No. Do you?" The minx had the audacity to reach down and run his fingers over his entrance. "Because I won't be satisfied until you're inside me and my stomach is covered in my cum."

It was impressive he already knew which buttons of mine to push. "That makes two of us." I moved to get lube and a condom out of my nightstand, before resettling between his legs once more. It was a challenge not to groan when he spread them wider to reveal all of himself to me. "*Mon dieu.*"

"I've got to say, I'm a big fan of the awe in your voice when you say that."

My anticipation grew as I teased his hole with slicked fingers. "How can I not be amazed by your beauty?"

He snorted in disbelief. "Yeah, okay. Uh-huh, sure you are."

I eased a finger into his tight heat, eager for more. "You do not believe you are beautiful?"

"At best, I'm cute in that boy-next-door, adorable

younger brother sort of way. Beautiful is some next-tier level that I definitely don't qualify for."

"You are those things as well," I told him as I took my time readying him. If he had not been with anyone since his breakup, I did not want to rush him. "But you are also *très beau*."

"No, the works of art we saw at the museum today were beautiful. Models like Rune Tourneau are beautiful." He shrugged. "I'm just me."

I added another finger to prepare him as I tried to convince him of the truth I saw in him. "If you were anybody other than 'just you,' I would not desire to ravish you as I am about to do."

He gave me a skeptical look. "You'd seriously pick me over someone like Rune? I find that hard to believe."

"I would take you over Rune himself."

Felix laughed, even as he relaxed into my touch as I kept working him open with waning patience. "Oh, that's complete and utter bullshit. No one in their right mind would ever choose me over Rune. Have you seen him?"

"I have more than seen him, and I still stand by my claim."

His jaw dropped as he propped himself up to look at me. "Holy shit, are you saying what I think you are?"

"That I have known all the pleasures that Rune has to offer?" I added a third finger, hoping to distract him and speeding things up. "There is not an inch of his body I am not intimately familiar with."

Instead of asking more follow-up questions, he

surprised me by collapsing back onto the bed with an agonized groan. "Fucking hell!"

"What?"

Whatever I had expected his protest to be, it was not him muttering, "Imagining the two of you hooking up is too goddamn sexy. It's super fucked-up that I could get off to a fantasy of my best friend's boyfriend and you together."

"That vivid imagination of yours seems prone to naughty thoughts." It was one of my favorite things about him so far.

"Oh, you have *no* idea," he said with a laugh. "Holy shit, I can't believe you dated Rune."

I was quick to correct him. "We never dated, because neither of us wished to be in a committed relationship. We had fun in our youth, but those days are long behind us. I am overjoyed he has found true love with his Callum."

That comment made Felix prop himself up once more to look down at me. "Wait, you know about Callum?"

"My brother keeps me well informed. Even if he did not, Rune also told me himself."

I did not like the hint of insecurity I saw in his eyes as I withdrew my fingers. "But you said those days were in the past."

"That is true of our intimacy as lovers, but he is still a dear friend."

Felix struggled to piece everything together. "Wait, so you two talk?"

"We reconnected after he began dating Callum. He has become good friends with your brother, so he was more comfortable with our friendship than he was in the past. I must admit, it was quite surprising to receive a warning from him about you. It was cute seeing him be so protective, but I of course had to tease him about it." The only thing cuter was the pleased grin on Felix's face.

"Seriously?"

"I would not lie to you. As Rune has become close with Augie and cares about you, he also cautioned me not to hurt you with my playboy ways."

He scowled at that. "I don't know whether to be touched, worried, or insulted that so many of my friends think I'm going to come home with a nasty case of jet lag and heartbreak."

"I am not interested in breaking your heart, *chéri*. My wish is for you to remember our brief time together with fondness, not regret." I captured his lips in a gentle, reassuring kiss.

"Then we're good." There was no fear or uncertainty in his expression, so I slid on a condom before pushing into him. I loved how his body yielded to me, welcoming me into his warm embrace.

He sighed as he relaxed his muscles. "Better than good, actually."

"We are only getting started."

His eyes lit up with excitement. "I'm very much looking forward to you helping me make up for lost time."

With great pleasure, I eased him into a gentle rhythm. "You are lucky I perform well under pressure."

"Something tells me you perform well no matter what."

I chuckled at his confidence in my abilities. "You are not wrong."

He looped his arms around my neck as he looked up at me. "It isn't hard to see that everything about you is exceptional."

I lifted his hips a little as I thrust into him with more vigor. "You are too kind."

"And you are very talented," he moaned, hitching one of his legs over my body to help me go deeper. "Feel free to talk dirty to me in French. Or tell me about what you fantasized about last night."

I humored him by saying in French, "*I pleasured myself while imagining all the ways I could make you moan my name. Why was I foolish enough to leave you alone last night?*"

He arched up under me with a needy noise. "Yes to whatever you asked."

I moved his leg up higher on my hip as I shifted positions. "It is unwise to agree when you do not understand what I said. It might be dangerous."

"You mean sexy dangerous?" He wrapped his other leg around me and hooked his ankles together for leverage to move. "Because I'm totally down for that."

"There is no danger in such pleasures, unless I dare to deny you when you were right on the edge."

His triumphant expression amused me. "Ha, I fucking knew it! You *are* into edging!"

"Was that something your fantasy version of me did to you?"

"No, but when you promised I'd enjoy your punishment—" He interrupted himself with a gasp as I guided his hips to allow me to push in deeper. "I predicted you'd be into it. And I was right."

I liked the sounds of that. "Congratulations on reading me so well. I am curious, though. What did you do to deserve my wrath?"

"You mentioned you couldn't wait to fuck me for real, and I joked I didn't realize I was such a glutton for punishment. In my defense, I thought there was no way in hell you'd actually want me."

"And yet, here we are, with me inside you." I punctuated each of my words with a hard thrust.

"Trust me, I'm celebrating the fact that you being balls-deep in me isn't going to be limited just to my late-night imagination. This is *so* much better than jerking off alone in the shower."

It was too much fun to tease him. "It would be even better if I edged you to make our pleasure last longer, *non?*"

His attempt at an innocent expression was ruined by a hint of a smirk tugging at the corners of his mouth. "Would you really deny me?"

"I would deny you nothing, *mon chéri*. I am not sure I could, even if I wanted to." There was more truth in my words than I expected. What was it about Felix that made me wish to give him the universe if that would make him happy?

"Is that so?" He reached down to stroke himself back to hardness as he watched me with a sinful expression. "You should be careful about admitting something like that. It makes me want to take advantage of you."

"By doing what?"

"I don't know. Demanding you kiss me or something."

More than happy to oblige, I leaned forward and braced myself on the bed to do as he requested. He cried out from the shift in angles as I kissed him with the full force of my passion. I craved more of him, burning with a fiery need for more of his spark that set my soul ablaze.

When we parted for air, I reached between us to work his renewed hardness. There was something heady about being the one who was bringing him to a new height of sexual pleasure. I moaned when his thighs tightened their hold on me as he writhed under me from the overload of sensations bombarding him.

As I put some flair into my stroke while thrusting hard, Felix cried out, "Oh, Arsène! *Fuck!*"

Hearing him crying out to me filled me with a strange burst of possessiveness I had no right to feel. Everything in me needed to hear him shouting my name again and again. I hoped it would satisfy the ache inside me that longed for him in a way I had never experienced before. If it did not, we both might be in danger of our hearts getting carried away by our passions.

How unexpected.

Chapter 5

Felix

I HAD NEVER BEEN HAPPIER to be impulsive and give in to what my dick desired. Arsène put my fantasies to shame with every thrust. To have an attentive and nonselfish lover was better than anything I had ever experienced, let alone imagined.

Every pump of his hips sent me soaring higher in a dizzying rush of ecstasy that left me breathless. The best part was whenever I called out his name, he growled mine in a masculine manner that made my toes curl in delight.

Blissed out of my mind, I raced toward my second climax. I rocked hard against him and then thrust into his hand, lost in the dual sensations that were almost more than I could handle. My muscles tensed as I felt that promising tingle that was about to overtake me.

Arsène swore in French as I tightened around him, which pushed me to my very limits. But it was hearing him moan my name that did it for me.

I climaxed with a shout as an explosion went off inside me of mind-altering satisfaction down to the very core of my soul. I couldn't breathe or think—couldn't do anything other than exist in the most powerful orgasm of my life that somehow got even better when Arsène came.

Guiding him closer, he gave me a tender kiss that left me dazed and wanting something I could never allow myself to desire. I could only whisper Arsène's name as I held on to him, not ready for it all to be over yet.

My last functioning brain cell reminded me what we were doing was nothing more than a casual hookup, so I needed to act like it. Speaking would be an excellent place to start, but the best I could manage was an amazed "*Wow*."

He smirked as he withdrew. "Indeed." To my surprise, he somehow reversed our positions so I was curled up on his chest as he rested under me.

"I don't know how the hell you did that, but I'm seriously impressed."

"It is easy when you are so boneless now."

"Way to make me sound like a chicken breast. That's *super* sexy." I laughed as I snuggled against him, enjoying listening to his heartbeat. "It's your fault."

Arsène wrapped his arms around me. I savored one of the best hugs of my entire life. He brushed his thumb against me as he continued embracing me. "I am more than happy to accept the blame for that."

"Well, I hope you're also ready for me to stay here, because I'm not moving again until you make me. And even then, I'm probably going to fight you about it."

He laughed hard, which filled me with a different kind of warmth than the sexual heat from before. "You are very welcome to stay here tonight, *chéri*. I am in no hurry to leave your side."

To distract myself from swooning, I teased him, "Oh,

I'm back to just *chéri* now? Am I only *mon chéri* when you're feeling amorous? Is that it?"

"Forgive me, I was trying to behave myself."

"You have my permission to not do that." I couldn't resist stroking his scruff, loving the feel of it against my fingertips. With my baby face, growing facial hair was impossible, which made his twice as appealing.

Arsène chuckled as he hugged me tighter. "Even if it is for a little while, I want to enjoy our time together." He kissed my forehead and melted me into a cooing puddle. So much for keeping my cool. "Can you blame me for wanting to possessively hold you tight?"

I liked the sound of that. "For the record, I'm totally on board for the possessive caveman thing."

"Why?"

"Because it makes me feel like you care." I cringed at how that came out, hiding my face as I nuzzled against him. "Not *you*-you, but boyfriends in general. Uh, not that you're my boyfriend, but—fuck it, you know what I mean. Anyway, my point is, it's nice to be wanted."

He caressed my hair, which soothed me as I became more mush than man under his touch. "It is a complete mystery to me that a boyfriend could not love you and only you with all of his heart. You are not mine, but I am already deeply fond of you and your bright spirit."

I groaned at his sweet words. "Why are you trying to make me fall for you?"

"Is that what you think I am doing?"

"No, you don't understand." I huffed in annoyance.

"That's the nicest thing a guy who isn't my brother or friend has ever said to me."

Arsène caressed my back, sending shivers through me. "Ah, that is no good, *mon chéri*. You need to develop better taste in men if that is true."

I snorted at that. "It's slim picking with guys my age. Everyone I try to date only wants to fuck around. It shouldn't be so difficult to find someone who is interested in a long-term relationship, yet I have four exes who couldn't run away fast enough."

The dark rumble in his voice sent a thrill through me. "Those bastards do not deserve you."

"Yeah, that's a real comfort when I'm sleeping by myself in perpetual singlehood, thanks."

He shushed me as he continued stroking my back. "You are not alone now. That must count for something, eh?"

"Minus the part where you've ruined normal guys for me."

"I will not apologize for that, either. You are worthy of far more than pathetic 'normal' boys who do not value your true worth."

But am I worthy of you? The question echoed within me, but I couldn't bring myself to say it out loud. I didn't want to ruin the heavenly experience of being in Arsène's arms. It was the closest thing to being loved I had felt in a very long time. Even though it was temporary, it was still nice that someone who wasn't my brother or a friend cared about me.

After enjoying an amazing dinner, I was becoming dangerously dazzled by all that was Arsène. I needed to find some imperfections before I fell for him like an idiot.

He glanced over at me as he wiped his hands on a towel after finishing the dishes. "You look like you are attempting to solve a great mystery."

"You're too perfect," I admitted because my mouth always betrayed me. "You have to have some flaw I'm not seeing."

"Such as being a Casanova who does not believe in love?" He smirked at me as he rested his hip against the kitchen counter. "Or perhaps I am terrible at returning texts?"

"You could save us a lot of time by simply telling me what's wrong with you." I scowled when he burst into laughter. "Hey, I'm being serious! It has to be more than you live far away."

Arsène approached me with a sexy swagger. "Is there some reason you are wishing I was less than perfect?"

"To help me keep perspective."

He hummed with interest. "What is your current perception of me?"

"That you're too fucking awesome," I complained, causing him to laugh again. "You're too charming, too gorgeous, and too damn talented for your own good. It's not fair!"

"Is that so? And what is the issue with *moi* being my *magnifique* self?"

I stood up from the kitchen table to face him. "You're going to get me into trouble."

Arsène reached out and pulled me into a loose embrace. "As I recall, you were *very* eager to get into 'sexy trouble' with me earlier."

"You might be more trouble than I can handle." Talk about understatements.

"Should I stop teasing you, *chéri?*"

He stroked under my chin like I was his kitten; it shouldn't have been so appealing. When he was giving me an out, I should have graciously taken it, but my dick overruled my common sense. "No, because I'm dying for you to kiss me again."

"Only kiss you?"

I swallowed hard, my heart hammering as I decided to go for broke. "And maybe fuck me senseless while you're at."

His soft smile as he traced my lower lip was too much for me. "Ah, you see? You have already uncovered my biggest flaw."

I blinked at him in confusion. "Which is?"

"That I can deny you nothing," he murmured before bending down to give me a teasing kiss.

I clung to him as he tasted me, overwhelmed by the lust he stoked within me. It made me hungry for more, but I made myself push him away. "If you keep kissing me like that, I'm going to want more."

"Then you are in luck, since I wish to give you more."

In a blink of an eye, Arsène swept me off my feet into a princess hold to carry me to his bedroom.

I looped my arms around him and held on tight, turned on by the show of strength. Not one to be easily defeated, I kissed up his neck to suck on his earlobe. I tried my best to sound sexy. "Give it to me good, Arsène."

The second I was on my feet, our hands fumbled with our clothes in between ardent kisses as we rushed to get naked again. Before I knew what hit me, he had me pinned facedown on the bed, covering my body with his. "Is this how you wish for me to give it to you?"

My sass went right out the window when I was so aroused by the possibility of him taking me hard. "Please!"

His dark, rumbling voice had a dizzying effect on me. "I love to hear you beg."

If that's what he wanted, that's what he would get. "Hurry, I need you in me," I whimpered, not the least bit ashamed of how wanton I sounded.

It did the trick, because he started working me open with two slicked fingers. "Does this displease you?"

"It's not enough."

Arsène spread them as a test. I did my best to stay relaxed, but it was difficult.

Since he was taking too long, I tried to speed things up. I clenched my muscles around him as I ordered, "Hurry up and fuck me, damn it!"

His chuckle sent shivers down my spine. "Commanding me instead of begging? Interesting choice."

Not getting the result I wanted, I started babbling. "Please, I want you, I need you, I—"

He didn't give me a chance to finish my sentence before his sheathed dick penetrated me to the hilt without warning. Arsène set a rough and fast pace that had me writhing under him in ecstasy. His fingers gripped my hips with the possessiveness that I craved as he gave me everything I wanted—right until he pulled out of me.

I glared at him over my shoulder. "What the hell? You're just going to stop?"

"Temporarily." He lay on his back and gestured for me to get on top. "I wish to see all of you, *mon chéri*."

There wasn't a world where I would complain about getting to go to town on him, so I shut my mouth as I guided him inside me again. "You could have said something first. A hard stop is just mean."

"*Pardon.*"

"I should get payback for that." Once seated, I didn't waste any time in moving.

Arsène watched me with a dark need that burned my soul with hellfire lust. "You would be punishing yourself, *non?*"

"Hey, don't start bringing logic into this!" I braced my hands on his perfect abs to balance myself as I rode him hard, loving how his body moved to meet mine with each bounce. "Maybe I'm secretly a masochist who would enjoy making us both suffer."

He laughed as he groped my ass to help guide my movements. "That is not how masochists work."

"A sadistic masochist might. You never know."

"You are far too demanding to be submissive. It is a delightful charm of yours."

I snickered as I pretended to be offended. "Wow, that's a really polite way of calling me an asshole. Thanks." Just to be a dick, I slowed down our rhythm as I let him almost fall out of me before sliding down again. "I could be submissive if I wanted to. Or did you already forget the part where I was writhing under you, begging for more?"

Arsène played dirty by running his hands up my thighs to get near my cock, only to deny me. "That is not a sight I shall soon forget. But ordering and begging are two very different things."

"Which do I need to do to make you touch my dick?"

The sexy jerk had the audacity to smirk at me. "Perhaps if you stop trying to torture us with this slow pace, I will indulge your desire for more."

"I'm only doing this because *I* want to." I picked up speed as I moved in search of a satisfying rhythm.

"But of course," he said in a tone of voice that clearly didn't believe me.

I reached down to give myself some relief, growling when he knocked my hand away. "Look, if you won't get me off—"

He shut me up by trailing his fingers along the underside of my cock. "Relax, *mon chéri*. I have no intention of stopping until you have decorated my abs with the evidence of your pleasure."

My laugh turned into a groan when he stroked me

with a loose grip. "What a fancy way to say you can't wait to see me blow my load on your stomach."

"That is a much more colorful phrasing." Mercifully, he gripped me tighter and jerked me off like he meant it.

I tossed my head back as I fucked him with wild abandon. "Oh, just like that! Fucking *yes!*" I got even louder when he added some flourish to his movements.

Arsène moaned my name and I damn near came from that alone. It became even harder to control myself when he spoke in French.

"I'm so close." My body tensed in anticipation of release. "Only a little more, and—"

He shifted the angle of penetration as he rubbed his thumb over the head of my cock, which fucking sent me. His name got caught in my throat as I came hard enough to see stars. It impressed me that my cum landed almost halfway up his chest.

Arsène didn't give me long to appreciate the view. He flipped me onto my back before I even knew what happened. He kept the fast rhythm I had set, which made me whimper from oversensitivity after my orgasm. My hands sought his shoulders as my thighs squeezed his sides.

He pushed in to the hilt, moving forward to capture my lips in a heated kiss as he came deep inside me with a satisfied moan. It did dangerous things to my heart, especially when he smiled at me with fondness while caressing my cheek with his clean hand. He murmured something in French with a gentleness that made my heart flutter like an army of hummingbirds taking flight.

"Did I make you come so hard that you forgot English?"

The deep rumble of his laughter sent shivers through me. "Almost."

"Care to translate?"

He slipped out of me, leaving me empty without him. "I said you were more tempting than the sweetest of cakes and far more satisfying."

His words suffused me with a warm glow. "Is that your way of saying you could eat me right up?" I yelped when he nipped at me.

"*Oui*, you drive me wild, *mon chéri*." He reversed our positions once more so I was on top of him as he hugged me like his favorite teddy bear.

I snorted in disbelief. "I'm sure you say that to all the guys you're with."

"*Non*, only you. It is not empty praise, but a confusing truth."

My stupid heart foolishly got its hopes up, so I dashed them myself before he had the chance to. "You find it confusing that you're attracted to me? Ouch."

Arsène guided me to look at him, allowing me to see how serious he was. "There is no mystery there when you are so cute."

"Then why are you confused?"

He stayed silent as he studied me, almost as if he was trying to see through me to find an answer. I thought he wouldn't reply, but he finally spoke in a soft voice. "Because for the first time, my heart has an opinion, and I do not know what to make of that."

Everything warned me not to ask, but I needed an answer. "What is it?"

"That it is going to hurt when you leave."

I didn't know how to respond to that, so I kissed him with a desperation that hopefully told him he wasn't the only one who felt that way.

Damn it.

Chapter 6

Arsène

It was not the entire truth when I told Felix that my heart's opinion was it would hurt when he left. The mere thought of our parting in a few days made it ache in a way I had never experienced before. It already felt like his return to America would bleed my world of all its vibrant colors. Why did it seem like I would lose my reason to laugh and smile when he was no longer by my side?

How had Felix become my joy in just two days? How was it possible that in less than forty-eight hours, my heart had learned to live only for him? Was it not madness to want to hold him tight and never let him go again? To feel like I could never be happy again if he left me?

I was a grown man of almost thirty-eight, who never had any problems enjoying amorous fun without my heart ever taking notice of my partner. How could I possibly explain why I desired to keep Felix and embrace him with all that I was in the name of love?

Nestled at my side, I stroked his hair as if he were a cat, smug in the knowledge I had worn him out. He may have the vigor of youth, but I had the stamina of experience.

It was unheard of for me to stay in bed and do nothing, yet there was nowhere else I would rather be. Embracing Felix brought me a sense of peace I had never known. It was yet another wonderful thing that would disappear from my life when he returned home. The thought made me hold him a little tighter, causing him to murmur in his sleep. I pressed a gentle kiss against his forehead, before resting my cheek against him.

I had always prided myself on being a generous lover, willing to do anything my partner craved. Making others feel great was part of the pleasure for me. But with Felix, for the first time in my life, I desired to be selfish. I wanted to take all he would give me so he would be mine, and mine alone. I wished to be the only one to make him cry out with lust as he climaxed. But he was destined to go home, where someone would never be as good to him as I could be. The thought left me with an unsettling discomfort.

It startled me when my mobile rang in my pants pocket across the room. Since it was after one in the morning, whoever was calling must have had an important reason.

I tried to detangle myself from Felix, but he clung to me with a sleep grumble that was precious beyond compare. Whispering an apology, I freed myself in time to answer on the last ring.

Before I could say anything, I heard a panicked "Where is he? Is he okay?"

I was careful to keep my voice down so as not to disturb Felix's slumber. "Is who okay?"

"Felix! Is he still with you? Please tell me he isn't out by himself this late at night."

The pieces clicked into place for me as I remembered Felix mentioning he had given my number to his brother for peace of mind. "Ah, you must be Augie. *Oui*, he is safe and asleep. Please rest easy."

Augie heaved a sigh of relief. "Thank god. When he didn't let me know he got back to the hotel, I was afraid something had happened to him."

I heard an Irish voice in the background say, "I told you he was fine. Stop worrying about the lad so much. I'm not ready for you to worry yourself gray and turn into a sexy silver fox yet."

Augie fussed at his boyfriend, Brody, before suspiciously asking, "Wait, why is he asleep if he's not at the hotel?"

Since I knew better than to tell him it was because I had worn out his younger brother with multiple rounds of intense sex, I chose a more benign answer. "We spent many hours walking through the Louvre and town today. He was feeling the effects of jet lag, so we came to my place to rest since it was closer than the hotel. He fell asleep, and I did not have the heart to wake him to send him on his way. You have my sincerest apologies for worrying you."

Augie sighed again. "I'm sorry, I shouldn't have called you."

"You have nothing to apologize for," I reassured him. "As an older brother, I understand your need for him to be safe. I do not mind the call if it set you at ease."

"Thanks for being so generous with your time, Arsène. It helps to know he's with you and not getting into god knows what trouble by himself."

I smirked as I remembered how our afternoon had started with "sexy trouble." Clearing my throat, I refocused myself on the conversation. "It is my pleasure. You have my word that he is being well taken care of. I would never allow him to return to the hotel at this hour without me."

From behind me, I heard an aggravated noise that drew my attention. I turned to see Felix sitting up with an angry scowl as he demanded, "Is that my brother?"

"It is."

Both of them said at the same time in a clipped tone, "Let me talk to him."

Getting back in bed, I handed Felix the phone. It was hard not to chuckle when he resembled an annoyed kitten with his hair spiked up from sleeping. "You didn't have to call Arsène, Augie! I'm fine." There was a long pause before he sighed. "Brody, can you please talk some sense into him? I'm not that much of a fucking train wreck he has to babysit me from an ocean away."

I reached out to rub his back in comfort. He gave me an apologetic look as he mouthed, "Sorry."

Whatever Augie said next caused Felix's annoyance to return. "In my defense, I didn't mean to fall asleep without calling. I was—" He fell silent with a chagrined expression. His voice was resigned as he apologized. "Look, I'm sorry I worried you, but you need to quit assuming I'm dead in the Seine River because I didn't check in with you yet. I promise I'll touch base with you tomorrow. Can I go back to sleep now?"

They exchanged a few more words before saying they loved each other. Felix ended the call with a swear as he returned my mobile. "I'm so sorry my brother called you."

"It is no trouble. I understand his need to make sure you are safe."

He played with the sheets, unable to look at me. "I get it, but he's acting like I'm a hopeless disaster who can't take care of myself. It's embarrassing."

"Speaking as an older sibling, I believe his fears are of the world around you doing harm, rather than you hurting yourself."

He sighed as he looked at me with troubled eyes. "It still makes me feel like a shitty brother that Augie always worries himself sick over me. He does it about everything. When I first started driving, he had panic attacks because he was so convinced I was going to die in a car crash. I was more scared to tell him I had been hurt in my accident last year than telling Dad I totaled his car. It took *months* before Augie didn't insist I text him every time I drove somewhere to let him know I was safe."

I reached over to caress his cheek. "It is how he shows he loves you, but I understand it is not an easy burden to bear."

Felix nuzzled into my touch. "He's not always this bad. Normally, he's pretty chill, but this is the longest and farthest I've ever been apart from him. He's obviously not handling it well. I hate how it makes me feel guilty about being selfish for wanting to come here."

"You cannot let his anxieties stop you from living your life. He would not want that for you."

"I know he feels like he needs to take care of me because Mom died when we were young, but I wish he could do it with less worrying. But then I feel like an ungrateful asshole for not appreciating everything he's sacrificed for me. And for giving him plenty of reasons to legitimize his worrying about me."

"That is not a healthy way of thinking. You feel bad, then Augie feels bad that *you* feel bad, then you feel bad that *he* feels bad about feeling bad—it is no good, eh?"

That drew a small chuckle from him. "Wow, it's like you know us. That's exactly what happens."

"At some point, you will understand that to worry is to love someone."

"Wow, maybe it's because I'm jet-lagged as fuck, but that seems super profound. I should remember that for later."

"If your brother did not fret about you so much, you would think he did not care."

He smiled at that. "Yeah, I'd definitely be wondering if body snatchers came and swapped him out for a pod person if he didn't freak out over me not touching base with him."

"So you see, it is not bad for him to worry. He may be anxious, but he still trusts you enough to come here alone despite that."

"I'm not alone, though. I have you." Felix straddled himself over me with a smile that did nothing to persuade my heart to stop being enamored with him. "Thanks for reassuring Augie I was okay and in good hands."

I wrapped my arms around him in a loose embrace. "Actually, I refrained from using that phrase specifically so he would not get the right idea."

Felix surprised me by resting his head on my shoulder as he hugged me back. "Do I have to go to the hotel now?"

The words escaped me before I could stop them. "I would prefer you stay here with me instead."

He melted against me, sending us both to the bed as he stayed on top of me. "Thank you, Arsène."

"You are most welcome, *mon chéri*. Sleep, so we can have our fun later."

I grinned when I realized he had already drifted back into dreams. Stretching to shut off the lights, I held him once more. Left alone with my thoughts again, my words from earlier returned to me: "To worry is to love someone."

Was that why I was already concerned about never seeing Felix again after he went home? Was that why I fretted about how I would ever go back to the way things were before? The thought of a life without his laughter, smile, and bright spirit filled with me an unspeakable sadness.

It seemed impossible to fall in love with someone so quickly, but everything in me wished to make him mine. The unfamiliar urge baffled me almost as much. Commitment had never been something I had desired before, but for some inexplicable reason, I wanted to build a life together with him.

There was some terrible irony that several people had warned me not to break Felix's heart, but no one had told me it was my own that was in danger. Belatedly, I realized that was what my brother must have meant when he cautioned me not to play with fire unless I was prepared to make sacrifices for Felix.

I hugged him tighter. He may not be mine forever, but for the moment, he was my everything.

Chapter 7

Felix

THE FIRST THING I noticed when I awoke was that I was not alone. The second thing I realized was Arsène wasn't there. Panic rose inside of me as I stared at the tall, beautiful stranger, who was looking at me with curiosity. With his dark brown hair, delicate features, and elegant air, he could have been a model. He certainly looked like one in his flashy slim-fit teal suit paired with a navy shirt and a striped tie.

He didn't seem to pose an immediate threat, but I sure as hell wasn't comfortable being a bedspread away from being completely naked in front of him. Shit, how did you say in French, "Who the fuck are you?" Too frazzled to remember my remedial high school lessons, I demanded it in English instead.

The man's blue eyes lit up with delight in a way that made me clutch the sheets tighter around me. "Ah, so you are the American?" he asked in a lilting French accent.

He seemed to know who I was, but I still had no clue about him. "Who are you?"

"I am Armand Bellamy." The fucker said that as if that explained who he was and why he was in Arsène's bedroom. Shit, what if he was his boyfriend? The thought nauseated me. I backed away from him when he sat on the bed, careful to keep the sheets high enough to shield me from his interested gaze. "*Enchanté*. Arsène's eye is as fine as ever. Perhaps I can persuade him to let me join in your fun."

The man was stunning but absolutely not. "I don't know who you are, or why you're here, but you need to get out."

"And leave someone as cute as you alone in bed? *Non*, I think not."

My fear made my manners take a backseat. "I'm not asking you. I'm telling you to get the fuck out!"

Since I was as intimidating as a Pomeranian wearing a pink bow, he only laughed. "With such fire, no wonder he likes you."

As I was debating the merits of whacking him in his gorgeous face with a pillow to fend him off, Arsène entered the room with a malevolent air. My dick perked up when he barked something in French that sure sounded like, "Get the fuck away from my man or forfeit your life." It was extra hot since he looked sexy as fuck in his maroon blazer with a mandarin collar, tight white T-shirt, and jeans.

Armand was nonplussed by the reaction and retorted with something I *almost* thought I understood. "Wait, did you just say *plan à trois*?" I demanded, getting seriously pissed.

The man smirked. "Ah, so that phrase you know. Interesting."

"Armand, I will not tell you again. Leave us at once," Arsène told him in a commanding voice.

"When did you turn into such a prude?"

Arsène's warning glare got a rise out of my cock. It was super fucked-up I wanted to get in trouble so he'd look at me with such sexy sternness, but I had always been a little weird.

Sighing dramatically, Armand stood up to leave. "Fine, I can tell when I'm not wanted. I'll have to find someone else to appreciate my charm and good looks."

As he walked out of the bedroom, Arsène said something in French that made Armand hold his hands up in surrender as he sighed, "*C'est la vie.*"

I stayed where I was as Arsène escorted the man out. He quickly returned alone and sat on the edge of his bed with a concerned expression as he reached out to smooth away the worried furrow of my eyebrows. "*Je suis désolé*, Felix. That was not how I wished to wake you this morning."

"And how did you want to wake me up?"

"With kisses, croissants, and coffee," he replied, pressing a tender kiss on my forehead.

I tapped my lips with a grin. "You missed."

He chuckled before trying again, this time giving me a sweet kiss on the lips I savored.

"That's more like it. Now, will you please explain to me who the hell that was and why he was in your bedroom while you were out?"

Arsène ran his fingers through his dark hair, ruffling it in a way that did nothing to abate my hardness hiding under the bunched-up sheets. "Armand is my assistant. He was dropping off some prints I requested earlier."

"That explains who he is, but not the in the bedroom part."

"I forgot I had told him to come by this morning. Since I am prone to oversleeping, he was looking for me, only to find you." Arsène caressed my cheek with an apologetic expression. "I left to get breakfast to surprise you and forgot all about it."

If Armand was Arsène's assistant, it made sense he had a key to his place, but not his willingness to sleep with both of us. "He seemed quite put out by me turning down his offer for a threesome."

"He is, how do you say? A hedonist? He lives for pleasure."

"Does he regularly volunteer to have threesomes with you? Because that's kinda fucked-up when you're his boss."

Arsène looked sheepish, which was a surprisingly cute look on him. "He is my oldest friend from childhood. Boundaries mean nothing to him."

"Which means you've totally fucked before."

He impressed me by not looking away in shame. "I will not deny that there have been times in the past when we have been with each other to satisfy our lust. But it has never been romantic in nature, nor will it ever be."

I groaned, because much like the thought of Arsène with Rune, the fantasy of him with Armand was also alluring. "God, could you please try being less sexy? It's giving me a complex about how hot it is to imagine you fucking other guys."

He arched his eyebrows in surprise. "And you do not picture yourself joining in the fun with us?"

"No, because the last thing I need complicating my life is falling in love with two unobtainable men at the same time," I replied with a scowl.

"It is for the best."

I looked at him suspiciously. "What makes you say that?"

"Because I could not bear to share you with anyone else." The possessive growl in his voice made my hardness ache for his touch. "Armand does not deserve to watch you in the throes of passion. That pleasure is for me, and me alone."

I shoved hard at Arsène's shoulder as I complained, "Goddamn it, stop trying to make me fall in love with you!"

He blinked in confusion. "What have I done to upset you so?"

"I never should have told you I was a sucker for possessive cavemen types," I muttered, my stupid erection still standing at attention over his claim on me.

"It is not deliberate on my part." He at least had the decency to be contrite. "It is something you stir up inside me that makes me feel so selfish."

"Oh, so it's *my* fault that my dick gets hard and my heart gets stupid every time you act possessive?" I scoffed. "Gee, thanks. That *really* helps."

The spark of desire in his hazel eyes made it harder not to touch myself. "Is that what you are hiding under the blankets?"

"Well, when you kicked down the door and threatened Armand to get away from your man, or whatever the fuck you said in French, of *course* my dick is going to get the wrong idea. I didn't want your assistant to know that, though."

Arsène tugged at the sheets, but I held on to them. "Does that mean this whole time—"

"I've had a raging boner because I was so turned on by you kicking him out? Uh, yeah."

He forced me back on the bed with a roughness that excited me. It was impossible not to get swept away by his hungry kisses that claimed my lips with burning need.

Despite my refusal to relinquish my hold on the sheets, Arsène snuck his hand under them to work my erection. I finally let go of them in favor of entangling my fingers in his hair.

Arsène tossed the covers off me to give me a blow job that had me almost shouting from how good it felt. It didn't take long for me to come when combined with the way his fingers dug into me with possessive need.

I may have climaxed, but I wouldn't stop until he did, too. With effort, I pushed him onto his back, allowing me to strip him of his jeans and briefs, as he took care of his jacket and shirt.

It was my first up-close glimpse of his uncut cock. We had always moved on so fast with me as the center of attention that I hadn't noticed until now. "Um, not to sound stupid and unsexy, but do I have to do anything differently? I've only been with circumcised guys."

I appreciated he didn't laugh at me. "It is not so

different. When the skin moves over the head, it feels good, which it will do on its own as you go. Do not worry so much about technique, eh?"

Since I had no choice but to take his word for it, I shrugged and started exploring his body first. It was like worshipping a masterpiece as I caressed and kissed him all over. I loved his small dusting of chest hair and the dark happy trail that led down to temptation.

Ignoring my trepidation over how different giving a blow job would be because of his foreskin, I gave myself a pep talk that I was capable of rocking his world. Taking him in halfway and getting him nice and wet, I did my best to move his foreskin as I slid him deeper into my mouth. It earned me a sexy French swear, which gave me a confidence boost. I got more into it once I realized I wasn't doing it wrong or hurting him. With great relish, I sucked his dick like I was born to do it, earning sexy sounds for my efforts.

When he growled, "*Nom de dieu*," I stopped. That earned me the closest thing to a glare I had received from him. Of course, he just *had* to make being annoyed sexy, didn't he?

"Sorry, I couldn't tell if that was a good swear or a bad swear. Should I keep going?"

His answer came in the form of knocking me backward to pin me to the bed again. I whimpered when he brushed his arousal against mine with a lurid smirk. God, why was being held down by him so hot?

He took both of our erections in his hand and started stroking them together. "As much as I want to see you swallow my seed, I cannot resist taking advantage of us both being in this state."

I looked at him skeptically. "You'd rather frot than come in my mouth?"

Arsène's eyes fluttered shut with a groan as he thrust against me. "*Mon dieu*, your mouth can undo me, whether or not my cock is in it."

I lit up at the potential for fun. "Ooh, it sounds like someone has a secret weakness for dirty talk."

"With the angelic face of a cherub and the sinful mouth of a demon, you will lead me straight into the hellfire of temptation." He kissed me hard as he picked up speed.

Knowing I was affecting Arsène was one hell of a powerful aphrodisiac. Running my hands down his back to grab his glorious ass, I gave him my best seductive look. "I can't wait to taste your cum when you explode all over me."

His reaction was almost instantaneous as he came, shooting his load on my stomach. I was so damn close, but I held on long enough to be evil. I swiped some of it up with my index finger and said, "*Bon appétit*," before making a show of sucking it off my finger as I climaxed. "Mmm, what's the word for 'delicious' in French?"

Instead of answering me, Arsène kissed me hard to taste himself on my tongue. Even after two back-to-back orgasms, I still couldn't get enough of him.

"Don't worry. I saved room for the croissants," I said.

The warmth in his eyes as he laughed filled me with

happiness. It delighted me even more when he got revenge by licking our cum off my stomach.

"I like how you play dirty."

"And I will enjoy getting you clean once more." With those words, he whisked me off the bed for a quick shower before we could have a delicious breakfast of actual food.

I MOANED AS I enjoyed my first bite of the huge croissant Arsène had brought back for me. The buttery, flakey pastry was to die for. "No offense, but this is the best thing I've had in my mouth all morning." Thankfully, he took my joke in the spirit I meant and chuckled. "I mean, you're delicious, but this is some next-level goodness."

"You will not find a better croissant in all of Paris."

"Elias was right. I'm never going to be able to enjoy the small, dry ones at coffee shops. This puts those to shame. And it's practically the size of my forearm!"

"He spoke the truth."

I grinned as I took another bite. "Are you saying our American croissants are not up to your highbrow European standards?"

He gave a disdainful sniff. "It is an insult to call those *things* croissants."

Damn, I was digging the snobbiness. "Ooh, go off. I can't wait to hear this rant."

"A croissant should be flakey because of the lightness, not because it is a stale imitation of greatness."

"Keep going." I pulled off a piece of the pastry to pop into my mouth.

"How can it even call itself a croissant when it is the size of a baby's fist?" He scornfully scrunched his nose, which was fucking *adorable*. "It is a culinary crime."

"God, what is it about French arrogance that's so sexy?" I took another bite as I pondered the mystery. "Since when is snooty so hot? It's not fair. American arrogance is boorish in comparison."

"What is the word Isidore likes so much to describe that? Uncouth?"

"He's definitely called Wren and North that as he stared down his nose at their antics." I laughed at the memories. "Your brother's quite the haughty little prince."

Arsène's wicked smile made me hungry for something other than the best pastry of my life. "I told him his arrogance would help him fit right in when he moved to America."

"You say that as if you aren't equally or more arrogant," I said with an amused snort.

"Ah, why do you think I knew that fact so well?" We both laughed at his retort. "In my defense, I reserve my arrogance for my talent, which merits such an ego."

I couldn't resist adding, "Don't forget about when it comes to your good looks and shitty pastries."

"But of course."

"Oh, that reminds me of something I meant to bring up earlier before you successfully distracted me with said good looks and sexiness."

He radiated amusement. "It does?"

"When do you want to take pictures of me? I still need to hold up my end of our bargain."

He looked at me over the rim of his blue coffee mug as he took a sip. "You know I would love to do that without our agreement, right?"

I folded my hands under my chin as I batted my eyelashes with my most innocent expression. "Because I'm so gosh darn cute?"

He couldn't stop himself from smiling. "*Oui, mon chéri*. I have wanted to photograph you since the very first moment I saw you."

His words filled me with a happy flutter. "And what am I supposed to wear?"

"What you have on, or what is underneath," he said with a playful gleam.

"If we do a boudoir shoot, I can't show my friends, though."

The desire burning in his eyes made me flush with heat. "Those would be for us alone."

It was probably sad, but I liked thinking of Arsène treasuring photographs of me. "I'm not sure I'm okay with full frontal being preserved forever, even if it was private. That feels dangerous in a bad way. I can already hear Augie's voice hitting new octaves in outrage over me being stupid enough to take dick pics."

He chuckled as he sat his drink on the table. The way he slid his fingers through the handle to cup the mug made me squirm with memories of him doing that to me. "No, they would be tasteful, not crude. Things are far more tempting when they're hinted at, rather than on full display."

"Like a creative positioning of the sheets?"

"Precisely."

That didn't sound bad, then. "Why don't we start in the studio with clothes and see how that goes?"

His eyes turned to molten gold, burning me up with lust. "That sounds most agreeable."

Finishing the last bite of my amazing croissant, I steadied my sudden rush of nervousness. "Then, let's go do this."

Chapter 8

Arsène

Since Felix had no modeling experience, it was important for him to be comfortable in my studio. The best way to do that was to give him time to get used to the area. I gestured for him to stand in front of a white backdrop while I began readying my equipment.

He looked around with curiosity, which was preferable to apprehension. "It's much bigger than I expected."

"I need space not just to take photographs, but also to process and touch them up afterward. Normally, I have a team helping me, but I gave them the week off since I would be spending that time with you."

"Wow, talk about a nice boss," he said in an impressed tone. "Most bosses would make their employees catch up on work."

While the lighting was perfect, I pretended to adjust the rigging. "I do not believe in overworking my staff. Thankfully, I have the luxury of never taking on more work than I want, so I take full advantage of that."

"I guess when you're as famous as you are, you can choose who to work with and when."

Satisfied with the lights, I started on the diffusers next. "It is one of the better benefits."

"Must be nice." His wistful tone surprised me. "I

can't even imagine getting to live that kind of life, where you get to do whatever you want."

"In the future, you will have your own success with writing. It will allow you to write any book you please."

He scoffed in disbelief. "It's a lovely thought but totally unrealistic."

As I walked over to pick up my camera, I commented without thinking, "If all else fails, you could come work for me. I would give you plenty of time to write."

"It's kind of you to offer, but that dream would quickly become a nightmare."

That was not the response I had expected to receive. "What makes you say that?"

Felix started ticking his points off on his fingers. "Well, for starters, I'd have to learn French. If my grades in high school were any indication, that would be an unmitigated disaster. Especially when combined with not knowing anything about professional photography. Throw in my brother losing his shit at me living so far away from him, plus the inevitable mess I'd make, thanks but no thanks."

Although I should have accepted his reply as a reasonable reaction, I made counterpoints. "Learning French is not so difficult. I could tutor you."

"Hi, have you met me? Because if you think I could take language lessons with you and keep my clothes on without a hard-on, you don't know me very well."

The thought of sexy tutoring stirred my desires once more, but I ignored it. "You would not need to speak

French to work here. All my employees are fluent in English because of my international clientele."

"Which is fine, right until I step foot outside and have to function in this city by myself with language skills comparable to a toddler."

It was a valid point, so I shifted to his next argument. "I do not understand what you meant by the 'inevitable mess' you fear."

He gave me a skeptical look. "Really? You can't think of a single thing I could do to fuck everything up?"

"I can replace broken cameras. It is nothing to worry about."

"It's not the camera I'm afraid of breaking."

The self-conscious way he said that made me realize what he was most worried about breaking was his own heart. The heavy sentiment hung unspoken between us, so I did my best to redirect the conversation to a safer topic. "I am going to take some test shots to ensure everything is correct. Do not worry about posing for these."

Felix shoved his hands in his back pockets. He looked extra boyish in his jeans and aqua T-shirt. "I'm not sure I know how to pose. Anytime someone tells me to smile for the camera, I lose the ability to control my face. I end up looking like I'm being held hostage."

"It is more common than you think." I snapped my first shot of him in profile, then took several more in quick succession. I reviewed them on the screen, pleased with the lighting. However, I pretended to adjust the settings on my camera by cycling through the menu to give him some more time to acclimate.

"So, what should I do?"

I held his gaze as I told him, "The best thing you can do is chat with me. Forget about the camera. I am not interested in a forced pose. I wish to capture the real you."

He grinned at my words. "You make it sound so easy."

"What is easier than being yourself?"

Felix shrugged. "What should I talk to you about?"

"Anything you please." A lot of photographers liked to make their uncomfortable subjects talk about themselves to relax. In my experience, being the center of attention for both the conversation and the camera was counterproductive. Having them focus on me instead led to them forgetting themselves. "You are welcome to ask me questions. Nothing is off-limits."

His green eyes brightened at the prospect, which I took a picture of. "I can ask about *anything*?"

"*Oui.*"

"Why do you never use contractions when you speak?"

I had expected a far different question. "In my line of work, the formality of my speech is one way I create an elegant environment."

"But you don't use them when it's just us and you're not working."

I once again pretended to adjust my lighting so he would continue thinking I was merely testing. "It is my preferred manner of speaking at this point. I am surprised that is the first thing you wished to ask me about."

"Izzy uses them, so I was curious why you don't."

"He is fifteen years younger than me, so he grew up with the internet. He is far more accustomed to using slang."

Felix took his hands out of his back pockets and moved them to the front ones. "That makes sense, I guess. What about in French, though? Are you more formal with it, too?"

"I am, although Isidore is not." Since he was distracted, I snapped another shot of him. "Would you prefer me to speak differently around you?"

"No, the elegance of your language suits you." He folded his arms over his chest, then uncrossed them again. "What the hell am I supposed to do with my arms?"

I had to bite the inside of my lip to stop myself from chuckling. "Whatever is natural."

He shook them out as if preparing to exercise. "See, this is what I'm talking about. You start taking pictures, and I forget what my arms are for. It just feels so *awkward* to have arms. Where do I put them?"

I did not want him to become fixated on the issue, so I suggested, "Would you be more relaxed sitting?" I pointed to the far wall. "You may use a chair if that is more natural for you."

"It's worth a shot." Felix went over to pick up a black wooden one and bring it over. He flipped it around to straddle himself over it, resting his forearms on the back of it. I captured his pleased expression. "Thanks, that's much better."

His position inspired a tempting fantasy about

receiving a lap dance from him. I forced myself to ignore it and take a few more snapshots instead. "I am glad you are more comfortable."

He spread his legs further apart as he slid forward in the seat, embracing the chair back. It gave me vivid reminders of them wrapped around me as he held on to me while I pleasured him. I shot a few more pictures of that glorious view to enjoy for later.

Unaware of where my mind had gone, he asked, "Do I get to keep asking you questions?"

Moving to get a different angle, I took a few more shots before answering. "You may ask as many as you like."

"Have you ever had a threesome with Armand?"

I snapped a picture of his ornery smirk. "No, despite his repeated offers."

"Really?"

"Why does that surprise you?"

"Because you're sexy as fuck—and I say this with no shade—but I get the impression you've had a lot of partners. Threesomes seem like a natural extension of that, and he seemed *very* convinced you'd share me. Plus, he's fucking hot, when he's not scaring the shit out of me first thing in the morning."

I continued taking more shots at various angles. "That was nothing more than his wishful thinking. I prefer to give one partner my all than divide my attention and risk someone feeling left out."

Felix rested his elbow on the chair back as he

propped his chin up on his hand. "When you say, 'give one partner your all,' do you mean only as a top?"

I took a rapid-burst series of his new pose. "*Oui*. My preference has always been to be the person giving pleasure."

"Are there ever exceptions?"

"Of course. If the best way to please my partner is to receive their attention, then I am open to that experience."

My answer made Felix shift in his seat as he bit his lower lip. I hoped my shots of that pose came out well, because I loved that expression on him. "You look like you wish to ask a follow-up question but are not sure if you are allowed to."

"That's because it's super inappropriate, but my brain is dying to know the answer."

"Are you wondering if I would give myself to you?"

I captured his flush of arousal in my next picture. "Okay, that's my second follow-up question."

"Then, what is your first?"

"I *really* don't want to say."

There was only one other thing I could think of that he might be curious about. "Ah, so you wish to inquire about my time with Rune. Are you perhaps wondering who was in what position to make your fantasies more realistic later?"

"It sounds *so* bad when you put it that way." He hid his face in his hands with a groan. "Sorry, I swear I'm not trying to be a pervert. It just confuses me because you both seem like tops who would never switch. Even with my vivid imagination, I can't picture Rune bottoming for Callum, you know?"

His curiosity amused me. "I cannot speak for their relationship, but he was the rare exception for me."

"Meaning?"

"I never took an active role with him." I snapped a few shots of Felix's stunned expression. "All I will say is that I never regretted giving up control to him."

Felix hesitated before asking, "Do you ever regret giving *him* up?"

"No, because his heart was never mine. We had our fun, but that was a long time ago. He has never been as fulfilled by love as he is with Callum. I am truly happy for them both. Please believe me when I say I have no regrets about how our sexual relationship ended, nor any complaints about our platonic friendship we have now." Felix still seemed uncertain, so I made myself explicitly clear. "I was fond of Rune during our time together, but there was no romance or feelings between us. It was only about physical lust and a mutual appreciation for each other's aesthetics. We are merely old friends at this point, nothing more."

Instead of clearing things up for him, Felix seemed more confused than before. "How is that possible? He's one of the most beautiful people alive, funny, an amazing cook, so incredibly kind—the list goes on and on. How did you not fall for him after being intimate together?"

I lowered my camera to give him my full attention. "Because neither of us were looking for love, and he was incapable of it back in those days. He was a much different person in the past, who did not freely laugh or express himself. His true self was buried, waiting for Callum to help him grow into someone capable of loving another with all of his heart. I wish them both all the happiness love can bring."

He remained silent for a moment before softly asking, "What about you?"

"What about me?"

"You said Rune was incapable of love in the past, but what about you? Are you capable of loving someone?"

"In the past, I had no use for love when I was only chasing after pleasure. I see things differently these days." The hopeful look in his eyes made me ask a question I should have kept to myself. "What about you?"

Felix hugged the chair as he rested his chin on it. My photographer's instinct snapped a shot of the moment. "All I want is to be in love, but I keep falling for all the wrong guys because I go for the first guy who shows any interest in me."

"What is it about love that is so important to you?"

He was quiet as he reflected on his answer. "I guess it's because after losing Mom, I understand how quickly someone can disappear from your life. If I died tomorrow, it's tragic that I've never known what true love feels like. Almost everyone I'm friends with is in a loving, fairy-tale relationship, so I feel left behind. I mean, *North* fell in love, and he didn't even believe in it until he met Elias!"

His explanation told me a lot about his experiences in life. "Rune did not either until he met Callum. If I have learned anything, it is that love finds us when we least expect it."

The long look we shared brought up a confusing mix of emotions. The pressure in my chest tightened when he asked, "Have you ever been in love before? With all of your heart, where that person is your entire world?"

I chose my words carefully. "In the past, I used to think the answer was no, but now, I am not so certain of that."

"What changed?"

My truth came out, unable to hold itself back from him. "I met you."

His eyes went wide as his breathing hitched. "What are you saying?"

"Something I probably should not."

"Please tell me."

I stood before him, my heart pounding as I cupped his flushed cheek in my hand. "It would be cruel of me to say."

"Please, Arsène."

The wise thing to do would have been to move on, but I could deny him nothing. I admitted what I had been struggling with earlier when I was alone with my own thoughts. "I wish you could be mine." His mouth dropped in shock, but I could not stop the words now that they had broken free of my soul. "I cannot stop myself from wishing I never had to give you up. My heart selfishly desires all of you when you can never be mine. I cannot bear the thought of another man touching you, but you are not meant for me."

Felix whispered my name as he stared at me with deep emotion.

My confession continued to pour out of me. "I have no right to crave you the way I do, but that does not stop me from wishing things were different. I am not sure if that is love, but you have not even left yet, and I already miss you more than the air I breathe. You must return to your life, but I do not know how I will make myself let you go. Every second we spend together makes it that much harder to lose you."

He teared up at my proclamation. "How do I not fall in love with you when that's the most romantic thing anyone has ever said to me?"

"I am not the one to ask when I seem to have already lost the battle against resisting your charm."

"But we aren't allowed to be in love!"

I smiled wanly at him. "It appears my heart does not care about that."

"How can I prevent myself from falling for you when that's how you feel?"

"*Pardon.* I was unprepared for you to captivate me so. You are too much temptation to resist, *mon chéri*. I realize now that I never stood a chance against you."

Felix took my hand in his as he looked up at me with desire. "If I'm going to hurt no matter what, then I want to savor every second of the good for as long as I'm here." His eyes beseeched me to give in. "You've already told me, but will you show me how you feel?"

I used his hold to pull him up from the chair. "If that is your wish, then I would love nothing more."

He interlaced his fingers with mine and squeezed my hand. "Lead the way."

It was sure to be a mistake, but nothing would stop me from pretending that he could be mine, even if it was only for a few more days. "Let me shut off the lights, and we can go."

Chapter 9

Felix

ONCE WE WERE BACK UPSTAIRS, Arsène said, "I feel like I should do the adult thing and stop this from happening."

Taking his hand in mine, I gazed up at him with a pleading expression. "I want to embrace whatever this is and enjoy it to the fullest. Even if it's only for a few more days, can we pretend this isn't ending when I get on the plane? Please?"

"But it will make it that much harder to let go."

It was a fair point, but I wasn't interested in listening. "Will anything make it easier?"

The corner of his mouth quirked upward. "*Touché*. If that is what you wish, then let us act as if we have the rest of our lives to enjoy ourselves together."

The kiss he gave me was slow and sensual as he staked his claim on me. I held onto his red blazer to steady myself as he sent fire shooting through my veins. His lips left no doubts about my status of being his. I whimpered when his hands slid under my T-shirt to caress my bare skin. Part of me wanted to beg him not to tease me, but the rest of me was enjoying the process of him demolishing my composure.

We stripped as we backed up closer to his bed. He

guided me to lie back as he caged me in place under him. I reveled in his attention as he kissed and caressed me all over, with just a hint of possessiveness that turned me on even more. The rough brush of his scruff against my skin made me squirm with need, my erection aching for his touch.

Before I could beg, his slicked fingers found my entrance and pushed into me. I gasped as he began orally pleasuring me while he readied me to take him. I did my best to memorize every detail of the glorious sight of him going down on me to enjoy later when I was alone in America.

When he brushed against that spot inside me, I cried out his name as I came. He put on a show of swallowing my release and licking me clean.

"There is no greater delicacy than the taste of your pleasure," he said in a dark, rumbling voice.

As he sat back, I ran my fingers over my entrance while giving him my best coy smile. "I want to feel you come deep inside me as you mark me as yours, Arsène."

"*Mon dieu*," he swore in a broken whisper as he stared, transfixed by my display as I slid a finger into myself while holding his gaze.

I intended to play on his weakness for dirty talk using his choice of words. "Take me with nothing between us. Fill me with your seed as you claim me as yours."

My words drew a strangled noise from him. It took him two tries to ask, "Are you certain this is what you want?"

"Without a doubt." I withdrew my finger with an

obscene squelch of the lube. "Please, Arsène. Take me. Make me yours."

My plea broke the last of his restraint. He guided my left leg to wrap around his waist as he lined himself up with my hole. I held my breath as he pushed into me without a condom on, exhaling once he was all the way inside me. He kissed me with need, trembling with emotions.

I gasped when he moved, stunned by the difference. The act was more intimate than before as he worshiped me with each thrust of his hips. I embraced him on all levels, clinging to him shamelessly as I moaned in ecstasy. It was the closest thing to making love I had ever experienced, and I was greedy for more. I wanted the moment to last forever, because being his was the best feeling in the universe as he looked down at me with unguarded adoration. For the first time, the true love I had always searched for was in my grasp. I wasn't about to let it go because of an inconvenient ocean separating us.

Although I could see it in his eyes, I needed to hear him say the words. "Please tell me, Arsène."

"Tell you what?" He reached between us to work my aching hardness. "That you are my everything?"

I squeezed him tighter as I raced toward my peak. "What else?"

"That I can only be happy when you are near?"

I keened as I teetered on the edge of release. "Say the words I've waited my entire life for someone to mean."

Arsène held my gaze as he murmured, "*Je t'aime, mon amour.*"

That did it for me. I climaxed hard, then pulled him closer for a hungry kiss. "I love you, too."

My confession drew his orgasm as he pushed in deep and came. Hugging him tighter, I let myself get caught up in the feelings I had promised myself I wouldn't catch. Going home with a broken heart for a souvenir would suck, but in that moment, I had never been happier or felt more loved.

When Arsène had cleaned me up, he surprised me by grabbing a camera instead of getting into bed. I couldn't resist teasing him about it. "Is this the part where I'm supposed to pose like a sex kitten for you?"

"I would enjoy a demonstration of that."

Covering my bits with the sheets so they weren't on full display, I arched my back with my arms stretched behind me. I turned smug when I heard the camera shutter go off. "Do you like that?"

"*Immensely.*"

His reaction amused me, so I continued teasing him by touching myself before I pretended to lower the sheets near my dick. Every click of his camera stroked my ego, but I still felt a little silly. "God, I probably look ridiculous doing this."

"*Non*, quite the opposite. You are *très* sexy."

I snorted in amusement. "Only you and my roommate think that."

A dark look passed through his eyes that made me bite back a moan. "Your roommate?"

"Ooh, somebody's jealous." That shouldn't have made me so happy, but it did.

"You seem unbothered by his interest in you."

I rolled onto my side, careful to make sure the sheets didn't slip down far enough to give away all my secrets. "He's never hidden the fact he thinks I'm hot and would have loved to nail me. But he's a good enough friend to know I needed more from a partner than he could offer me, so he kept his dick in his pants. He would never stray from Elias now that they're together, so you have nothing to worry about."

"*Très bien.*"

"If you want to keep being jealous, I'm fine with that. Although," I told him with a playful wink, "it really gets me going."

He lowered his camera as he looked at me with a concerned expression. "So long as you understand it is not born out of a desire to manipulate you or cut you off from anyone. There is a difference between wishing you were mine and being abusive."

"That you care enough to caution me about that tells me everything I need to know," I told him. "When you say I'm yours, it's not in a 'no one else can ever talk to you, because you're my property' kind of way. It's the same reason I'd never tell you to stop being friends with Armand."

He looked relieved at my words. "We are of the same mind."

I crooked my finger and gestured for him to move closer. When he took a picture before complying, I had to laugh. "It's sexy how professional you are when you have a camera in your hand."

"Are the sheets hiding your arousal again?"

"Why don't you come over here and find out for yourself?"

Arsène approached the bed, taking more shots when he was in close range. "If you keep acting like this, it is going to further delay our plans for today. It would be a waste to not go out and see more of what Paris has to offer."

"Which means you're about two pictures away from jumping my bones?"

"*Oui.*" He clicked the shutter twice, then set his camera aside to join me in bed for another round.

AFTER A DELICIOUS LUNCH, Arsène and I walked through the Jardin du Luxembourg. The garden was stunning, especially the magnificent fountains and sculptures we passed as we wandered hand in hand. It was like a beautiful dream I never wanted to wake up from.

"Can I make a request for tonight?" I asked when we sat down in the grass for a break.

"Of course."

"Would it be okay if we stayed at my hotel? I love your apartment, but I feel super guilty not using my room when I know my brother paid a lot for me to stay there."

His fond expression melted my insides to goo all over again. "I understand. We can spend the nights there for the remainder of your time here if you wish."

I leaned over to rest my head on his shoulder with a happy sigh. "Thank you. I really appreciate it, even though I hate asking. Your apartment is *so* nice."

Arsène wrapped an arm around me to hold me close. "There is no need to feel bad about such things. As long as I am with you, I do not care where we are. Perhaps you should video chat with Augie from the hotel tonight so he can see you there and not worry as much as last night."

"You wouldn't mind?"

He kissed my forehead. "Not at all. I will use the time to call my brother."

"Sounds great." It was amazing playing pretend like I was living my perfect love life with Arsène. "What are our plans for tomorrow?"

"We are going to the Palace of Versailles."

I perked up at the news. "Nice!"

"While I have not been in many years, it is well worth the trip."

"When did you last go there?"

He made an indecisive noise as he reflected on his answer. "Hmm, it must be at least ten years ago, maybe more. Rune wanted to do a photo shoot in the gardens, so I obliged him."

Knowing how fascinated Rune was by the French Revolution, I suspected he had ulterior motives. "It had more to do with him wanting to visit the palace than the photography, didn't it?"

Arsène chuckled. "*Absolument.* We had to take the tour before he would let me take any photos. In true Rune fashion, he ended up teaching the guide about some obscure points regarding the French Revolution."

I laughed at that. "Yeah, that tracks. He knows more about it than most experts in the field do."

Arsène brushed his thumb against my shoulder. "I do not doubt that. It will be fun to return with you. We shall see how much of his history lesson I remember."

"His poor students won't survive when he starts teaching next month at UC Berkeley."

"*Au contraire.* Rune may be an introvert, but he is a talented teacher," Arsène said.

I hurried to correct myself. "Oh, I wasn't talking about his abilities. He was great when we talked about things I could do here in Paris. I meant more the fact that his poor students are going to walk into class expecting to see a regular grad student. Nobody in their right mind would expect to learn French History 101 from the famous model who starred in the infamous elevator sex commercial."

That drew another laugh from Arsène. "Ah, that is true. No one is ever prepared for that. But I am confident that his passion for history will connect with them so they see the real Rune. It will be good for him to be back in academia once more."

"Agreed." Glancing around the park, I appreciated the beautiful view. "You know, this really is a wonderful city. I'm so glad I came here to visit. And I'm not just saying that because of you."

"I am pleased you are having a wonderful time during your stay here. It has been fun rediscovering the charm of my hometown through your eyes." He reached over and squeezed my hand.

"Thank you for being the best tour guide ever."

"It is my pleasure. There is still much to see. After this, we will visit the Palais-Royal. I believe you will enjoy it there."

I smiled at him. "I'm pretty sure as long as you're there, I'll have a good time anywhere we go." His pleased reaction filled me with warmth. "How long has it been since you've visited America?"

He stroked his chin while thinking. "I flew out to Sunnyside with Isidore when he moved out there to start school. That way I could help him get settled. I then headed down to LA for business for a few days in case he needed me to return for any reason."

"You're such a good older brother." It was one more thing I loved about him.

"I do my best, but sometimes I fear it is not enough. But Isidore has always been very independent, so I try not to worry so much. He knows I am ready to be on the next flight over if he needs me."

"Well, if you come out to see him, maybe you could spare a little time for me, too," I said in a hopeful voice.

Arsène reached over to caress my cheek with a loving look that made my heart stutter in my chest. "I could not resist such temptation. It is already hard enough not to fabricate reasons to visit my brother if it means seeing you again soon."

I nuzzled against his palm. "You have my permission to do that because I'm not ready to give you up yet. Izzy will probably forgive me for being a selfish bastard and stealing you away for a few hours."

"Ah, but I could not stop at hours, *mon amour*. If I followed you there, I do not know if I would have the strength to leave you once I had you in my arms again."

I swooned like a Victorian lady with the vapors over his romantic declaration. "For the record, I'd be fine with you never wanting to leave. Actually, that would be awesome."

"Indeed, it would be."

I shifted positions to cuddle at his side once more. It was an impossible dream, but I was determined to enjoy the fantasy for as long as I could. It was hard to ignore the ticking clock countdown on our remaining time together, though.

Chapter 10

Arsène

BACK AT THE HOTEL, I stayed in the living room suite while Felix talked to his family in the bedroom. To fill the time, I video called my younger sibling. He answered with a wave as he greeted me.

It was good to see Isidore's face again, even though it had only been a week since our last video chat. He looked great in a black, gray, white, and purple flannel button-down shirt. Felix's description of my brother as a haughty prince was an apt comparison. We both got our regal bearing from our mother's side of the family. I did not appreciate the implication of his knowing look. "What?"

"How are you enjoying playing tour guide? Is it as arduous as you expected?" His wide grin said he knew the answer to his questions.

"*Non*, it has been most enjoyable."

"Ah, so you have already fallen in love with him then, eh?"

I arched an eyebrow at him. "What makes you ask that?"

Instead of answering, he countered with a question of his own. "Do you deny it?"

"I do not understand why you would assume that."

"Because I've seen Felix's pictures. You're not that

good of an actor, Arsène. You obviously have feelings for him, despite my warnings."

I sat up a little straighter on the sofa. "And if I do?"

"What 'if' is there?" Isidore scoffed. "The only question is if it's love or lust, and even then, I don't think there's much debate there, either."

"What makes you so certain?"

He grinned. "Your refusal to give me a straight answer is a huge tip-off."

I scowled at that. "You warned me not to break his heart. You should not have been so cryptic when cautioning me about my own."

"The only way you could break Felix's heart would be by not reciprocating his feelings," Isidore explained. "You've never been able to resist a fiery spirit, and Felix is by far the feistiest. He's a perfect match for you, but only if you're committed to making it happen."

In hindsight, it was clear my heart never stood a chance of resisting him. "That is fine, but it does not change the reality of our situation being impossible."

Isidore pressed the back of his hand against his forehead as he feigned woe. "Oh no, if only you were a world-famous photographer who could work anywhere and had countless connections, plus a beloved brother who lived there."

"Are you suggesting I move out there to be with Felix? That is ridiculous. I cannot uproot my entire career on a whim."

He looked at me skeptically. "I'd bet money that idea becomes a lot less absurd after Felix leaves you to come home. I'll be shocked if you aren't on the next flight out here."

"Why do you seem so certain?"

"For the same reason you're so afraid: because it's the truth."

It was impossible to argue the point. Before I could respond, Isidore's roommate and best friend entered the room. As per usual, Wren was flamboyant with bright pink hair. His purple T-shirt had a white skull on it with red heart eyes and crossbones tipped with hearts. He draped himself over Isidore's shoulder as he said, "Hey, Arsène! What's up? Fallen in love with Felix yet?" Wren's physical affection was something my brother had secretly come to adore, although he would never admit it.

"Why does everyone think that?" I huffed in mild annoyance, despite it being true.

"Dude, it's because we have eyes and saw Felix's pictures. You're fucking *smitten*." He laughed at my dilemma. "Have you started looking for apartments out here yet, or are you still too deep in denial to be that pragmatic?"

It amazed me they both seemed so certain that I would do such a thing. It also shocked me that part of me was almost ready to give in and commit to doing it. The thought of losing Felix to the ocean between us was far too painful. "No, I have not made any decisions."

"You should talk to Rune, then," Isidore suggested. "I suspect his perspective would be the most helpful to you right now."

"Perhaps I shall."

"I look forward to seeing you soon," Wren said as he continued hugging my brother. "I can't wait until you move here."

"You know, we still have plenty of time to discuss the status of the relationship between you two." It was only fair for me to get a little payback by playing on their will-they-won't-they dynamic. "Perhaps you are ready to admit there is more between you than merely friendship?"

"I guess we could try making out and see what happens," Wren joked, earning an eye roll from Isidore, who shoved him away. "Aww, you're no fun, Iz. Why do you always have to shoot me down?"

"Because you never learn," Isidore retorted, barely able to restrain his amused reaction. "I refuse to make out with you to prove a point to my brother."

"Oh, but it's cool if we do it for the sheer hell of it?" Wren made kissy faces at Isidore, who grabbed the nearby pillow off the couch to hit him in the face with it.

Wren pretended to pout. "Damn, a simple 'no' would have sufficed, man."

"Since when?" My younger sibling returned his attention to me. "Call Rune, Arsène. We'll speak again once he's talked some sense into you."

We exchanged a few more words before I did as he suggested. Rune was in his office, looking handsome in his purple stand-collar button-down cardigan. He elevated it to elegance by pairing it with a black vest, tie, and white shirt. Amongst all the models I had worked with in my career, he was by far the most beautiful. The happiness he radiated from being with Callum made him all the more stunning.

"I bet I know why you're calling me," he said with a sly grin.

"To say hello to a dear friend?" Between dating Callum and befriending Augie, Rune had finally reached a place where he could accept my friendship I had always offered him from the first time we met. It was something I did not take for granted now that we were in regular communication with each other. "It is not so unusual these days."

He looked as if he did not believe me. "Is that the only reason?"

"What ulterior motive do you believe I have?"

"You've fallen for Felix and don't know what to do?" Rune laughed when my jaw dropped. "Thought so."

I ran my fingers through my hair with a scowl. "First my brother, then Wren, and now you? Am I really so obvious?"

"Sorry to break it to you, but from what I've seen of the pictures Callum's shown me, you're doing a shit job of hiding your feelings."

"It seems I need to look at what he has been posting. I was unaware I was betraying myself so openly. Can you send me an example?"

"Sure." Rune picked up his phone to text me a picture.

I opened it and saw it was one from our dinner at a restaurant near the Palais-Royale. Felix cuddled at my side as I held him, while we gazed at each other like two fools hopelessly in love. "*Merde.* I am in more trouble than I thought."

He chuckled. "I can't say I'm surprised."

"Why?"

"Because you find unusual people fascinating. You liked me because I was nothing like the other models you worked with. You're intrigued by Felix because he's a spitfire who challenges you, which you thrive on. His unpredictable nature is irresistible to somebody like you."

They were all valid points. "What am I supposed to do? I want him so much, but I cannot have him."

"If you stay in Paris, that's true."

I arched my eyebrows in surprise. "Do you also believe I will move to Sunnyside for him?"

Rune chuckled. "I think your first night apart will have you asking for my Realtor's info in the morning on your way to the airport for the next flight here."

"But that is madness! It has only been three days."

His expression became sympathetic. "That's how it was for me with Callum. It only took a few times of seeing each other for him to change me for the better. It baffled me that he turned me into a hugger by the third night we met in person after a lifetime of hating them."

That made me lean back in shock. Rune had always been particular about hugging, doing his best to avoid it at all costs. It was a preference I had indulged him with personally and professionally by never staging a shoot where he had to embrace other models. "That is quite impressive considering your history."

His happy smile told me more than words ever could.

"I thought I had lost my damn mind to consider dating someone, especially when he was so young. But not being with him was too unbearable. I couldn't handle the idea of another man hurting him, so I made my choice to make him mine. I haven't regretted it for a single second. Giving in to my feelings for him was the best decision of my life."

I glanced at the closed bedroom door with a worried frown. "My heart is ready to give up everything for him, but my mind is not as sure. To throw away what I have worked so hard for to be with a boy I barely know after a few days, it is..."

"On paper, it sounds nuts," Rune said. "But in reality, you're connected with plenty of models based in America, who will be thrilled you're stateside. I'm happy to do anything I can to help establish a studio here in Sunnyside. Plus, you can keep your Paris location and have Felix join you while you work there during summers and breaks. It's not as far-fetched as it seems."

I thought about what he had suggested. His plan had merit. Maybe it might be possible to have it all. "It sounds daft and too good to be true at the same time."

"I can promise you it would be worth it. Felix is a great kid, with a heart dying to love the right man. You're that person, Arsène. I have no doubts."

"Are you sure it would not cause problems for you and Callum if I am there? It is one thing when we are only in contact online, but in person might be different."

He shook his head. "No, we've had many conversations about that time in my life, so there are no secrets between us. He doesn't mind that we're still friends, because he's confident that my love for him is absolute. As amazing as you are, not even you could change that." There was a knock on his office door. "Speaking of which. Come in, baby. Say hi to Arsène."

Callum appeared, looking adorable in a sea-foam-green blazer, a lavender shirt, and white jeans. With his fair skin and red hair, he was angelic perfection. It was cute how he lit up with excitement when he saw me on the monitor. "Hello! How have you been?"

The lack of suspicion in his blue eyes told me so much about the trust they had built in their relationship. "I have been well. It is good to see you again." The last time we spoke had been when Rune introduced us over a call.

He didn't resist when his boyfriend pulled him onto his lap to embrace him from behind. "It seems like you're having fun with Felix."

"Your smile tells me you also think there is something more happening between us."

He fidgeted in Rune's hold. "In my defense, there's lots of photographic evidence that his feelings aren't one-sided."

Rune chuckled. "How diplomatic of you to put it that way."

"It would be grand if things worked out for them like it has for us. I want that for Felix, because he deserves to be loved for the amazing person he is."

Unable to resist, I ran Rune's idea by him as a hypothetical. "Even if that means I relocate to Sunnyside to be with him?"

To my surprise, he brightened at the prospect. "That would be so wonderfully romantic! Would you really move here for him?"

While Rune had told me it would be fine, it would assure me hearing it straight from Callum. "Would that bother you?"

It was precious that my question befuddled him. "Why in the world would that bother me?"

Rune answered for me. "He's concerned you would be uncomfortable with me working with him to establish a new studio here because of our past. We wouldn't want you to worry about us."

"Oh!" Callum seemed surprised by the idea. "Is it bad it didn't occur to me to be jealous?"

Rune hugged him tighter. "No, because it shows you trust me enough to believe I would never look at anyone but you. You're all I desire in this world."

Callum beamed with happiness. "I appreciate you being considerate of my feelings, but I'm fine with it. The past is the past. Rune loves me, and I'm pretty sure you feel the same way for Felix. What do I have to be worried about?"

"Your pure heart is a gift, Callum," I complimented him. "The world would be a much better place if more people saw things your way."

"Aww, thank you."

Rune grinned at me over his boyfriend's shoulder. "When are you going to tell Felix?"

"Tell me what?" Felix asked, startling me. I had not heard him enter the room. "Wait, is that Rune?"

I gestured for him to join me on the sofa. "Callum is here, too."

Felix waved at them as he sat down. "Hey, guys! How's it going?"

"Great! How much are you enjoying Paris?" Callum asked.

"It's *amazing*! I'm so in love with the city."

"Just the city?" Rune asked, getting an elbow jab from his boyfriend. "Hey, it's a fair question."

Felix blushed, making it difficult to resist the urge to pull him into an embrace. "No comment."

"Well, we should let you go since it's late over there," Rune said. "I'm sure you have a few things you still need to take care of before bed."

"I can't wait to hear all about your trip when you get back," Callum added. "It sounds like we'll have a lot to talk about."

Felix beamed at them. "We sure will. See you soon!"

After ending the call, I gave in to the urge to wrap my arm around his shoulder. "How are your brother and Brody?"

"Augie was relieved I called him from here, so that was a good idea on your part." He reached up and laced his fingers with mine. "I thought you were calling Izzy?"

"I spoke to him and Wren, but since I still had some time left, I called Rune for some perspective."

Felix shifted to look at me. "Perspective?"

"It was most helpful."

"How so?"

I brushed my thumb against him as I tried to figure out how to answer. "It helped me see things a little more clearly."

"Are you going to keep being cryptic, or can you give me a clue?"

"That depends on how you feel."

His quizzical expression was adorable. "Okay, you've officially lost me. Is your answer contingent upon me confessing a deep, undying, eternal love for you or something?"

"There would not be much point in me relocating to Sunnyside if you did not want me there."

He stared at me with wide eyes. "Wait, wait, wait —*what*? Are you serious? Tell me you're serious and not fucking with me."

I pulled Felix to straddle my lap so we could look each other in the eye. "*Mon amour*, I would never do that about something this important."

"Sorry, I wasn't implying that you were, but you can't be serious, can you?" He looked scared to believe me. "Why would you do that?"

"Because losing you will steal all the joy from my world," I told him. "My brother and Rune are correct that my job gives me the flexibility to take photographs anywhere. Should I wish to start a second studio in Sunnyside, it is not beyond my means. Rune has also offered to assist me with his connections. We could return here during your breaks."

"You're not talking in hypotheticals, right? You mean for real?"

I caressed his back to comfort him. "Many things would have to happen first, but it is an idea that I am willing to make a reality if you—"

Felix didn't give me the chance to finish my sentence. He threw his arms around me in a bear hug, trembling with the force of his emotions. "I know I'm a selfish asshole, but if you're serious—I don't have words for how happy I would be."

Holding him tighter, I was at ease with my decision. "I will make it happen if it means I can be with you."

"I'm so happy," he whispered, his voice cracking with his emotions. "You'd really do that for me? Even though it's only been a few days?"

"*Oui*, I have never been more certain of anything in my life." As I held him in my arms, I would do whatever was necessary to keep him there forever.

As our kisses started getting more heated, it surprised me when he pulled back with a concerned expression.

"What troubles you?"

He fidgeted in my lap. "Um, I don't want to disappoint you, but..."

Caressing his hair, I told him, "You could never do that."

"Shit, there isn't any way to say this without it being super awkward."

"Tell me."

Felix took a deep breath to steady himself. "Okay. I'm just going to say it, awkwardness be damned. I want to be with you tonight, because your surprise news about maybe moving to Sunnyside was incredible. Plus, sex with you is mind-blowingly amazing."

"But?"

He bit his lower lip as he hesitated. "But the thing is, since I've been single for so long, I was woefully out of practice before coming here. I'm definitely feeling it now. It's the good kind of sore, but I want to take full advantage of tomorrow being our last night together, so—"

"Ah, I understand. There is no need to feel bad about that."

"Like, don't get me wrong. My spirit is *very* willing, but my ass needs a break from your enormous dick for a night to recover."

It was impossible to stop myself from laughing. "What a problem to have, eh?"

"Try not to let it go to your ego." His expression turned sensuous. "I'm not saying we can't do other things, though."

I wrapped my arms around him in a loose hold. It was important that he understood our relationship was not purely about the physical. "What if all I want to do tonight is cradle you in my arms as you drift to sleep?"

"One, you're a dirty liar. Two, are you seriously telling me you don't want me to suck your dick right now?"

"The sight of your beautiful lips wrapped around my manhood is among the greatest joys I've known in this life," I told him. "But I do not want you to think you must pleasure me to keep me interested in you. Holding you brings me as much happiness."

"You're totally cool if all we do is cuddle tonight?" Felix still seemed suspicious. "That's not too boring to you? It doesn't feel like a waste of our limited time together?"

"Time spent with you is never a waste. Memories of having you in my embrace will keep me company on the nights we are apart. I do not want only sexual gratification from you. Being near you is enough for me."

He kissed me with fervent passion, allowing me to feel his hardness pressing against me. When I laughed, he scooted back with a groan. "Fuck, sorry. My dick is so stupid."

"Why do you say that?"

"Because it's like, 'Wow, I'm *so* turned on that he doesn't want to fuck me tonight,' which makes zero sense," he complained. "I've never been with a guy who's as down to cuddle as to fuck, and it turns out that's a huge turn-on for me. Now I'm torn between enjoying platonic hugs and getting my rocks off, which defeats the point of you being respectful enough to do nothing. Stupid dumbass dick and its mixed messages, ugh."

I snickered at his dilemma. "What do you wish to do?"

He gave me an exasperated look. "Do you really think I'm capable of making a rational decision when I'm dying to nut?"

"Dying to nut?" I shook my head at the strange phrase. "That is a new one for me."

"It means I want to rub our cocks together until we both come on your stomach or mine. I'm not picky. I just need you touching me until I explode. Think you can do that for me?"

My own arousal responded to his vivid description. I gathered him into a hold and carried him to the bedroom. "*Absolument, mon amour.*"

The instant I put him down, he shed his clothing so fast, it was as if they had combusted off him. I chuckled at his eagerness as I stripped out of my own. When he pushed me back onto the bed, I did not resist as he scrambled on top of me.

Felix braced himself on his hands as he leaned forward to kiss me, whimpering as he rubbed his hardness against mine.

It was a novel experience to have him rutting against me with blind lust. I caressed him all over as his hips picked up speed. He rocked against me with needy noises that drove me wild. I savored the beautiful view of watching him get off from such simple pleasure.

Unable to resist the temptation, I brushed my fingertips over his pucker. He keened and thrust back against me. Rather than penetrating, I continued teasing him with a hint of it before backing off.

He groaned with frustration. "Arsène, I'm so close, please, just a little more!"

Reaching between us, I took both of our erections in hand to stroke them together. Three tugs were all he needed to draw his orgasm. Him coming on me was enough to push me over the edge. I moaned his name as my seed mixed with his on my stomach.

Only then did he stop his frenetic movement. He pushed me to my limits when he shifted lower into a position that allowed him to lick our commingled releases off my skin. The sensual sight was seared into my soul forever as he murmured approvingly.

"God, I feel *so* much better," he sighed in relief. "Sorry to ruin your romantic gesture of 'not having to do anything sexual to be satisfied' plan."

I pulled him into my embrace. "You have ruined nothing, *mon amour*. As long as you are happy, that is all I care about."

He melted against me in a boneless puddle. "*So* happy."

"As am I." Never in my life had that been truer for me. When being with him was so incredible, a move across the ocean to be with Felix did not seem so foolish. It was the best decision I had ever made.

Chapter 11

Felix

As we walked through the gardens after our incredible tour of the Palace of Versailles, I wasn't my usual talkative self. Thus, it didn't come as a surprise when Arsène asked, "Is something wrong?"

I shrugged. "I'm not sure 'wrong' is the right word for it."

"Then which is?"

We stopped in front of an impressively large fountain with four horses emerging from the water and the god Neptune in the middle. "I don't know. I'm just in a weird headspace."

"Do you want to talk about it?"

Taking a deep breath, I did my best to sort through my feelings. "I'm having an awesome time here, but I'm sad I'm leaving tomorrow. Part of me wants to stay here forever, but I also miss my brother and friends. I want you to hug me and tell me everything is going to be okay when I go home. But I also need you to pin me to the mattress and fuck me so hard I'll feel it for the next week as a physical reminder this happened."

It tickled me when he whispered under his breath, "*Mon dieu*," at my declaration.

"I so badly want to believe you'll move out there, but

I'm scared to get my hopes up. I've never been happier and sadder at the same time, so it's kinda fucking me up in the head." I kicked the ground with the tip of my shoe. "I'm not ready for this to be over yet and go back to real life."

Arsène guided me to look up at him. "Just because you are going home does not mean this is over between us. I need to make arrangements here so I can leave and arrange a place to stay in Sunnyside. However, I have no intention of not talking with you while I do so. We can video call every night until I move."

It helped to hear, but I worried it was too good to be true.

His voice was gentle as he continued reassuring me. "You have nothing to fear, *mon amour*. I am not letting you go now that I have found you."

My anxieties lessened when he returned my hug. "I'm sorry I'm scared. It's not because I don't trust you. You're the best thing that's ever happened to me, but I'm used to disasters blowing up in my face."

He held me tighter as he rested his chin on the top of my head. Considering I was tall, that was no small feat. "It is okay, Felix. The unknown is always a little scary. But you have my word I will do everything in my power to be with you as fast as I can. I do not wish to spend one more minute apart from you than I have to."

Annoying niggling doubts ate away at me. "But what if I go home and you realize you were only caught up in the moment and don't want to be with me anymore?"

"Listen to me, not your fears. This is not a passing

fancy. You are my heart, and I cannot live without you. I will tell you that as many times as you need to hear it."

"But won't you get sick of doing that and think I'm just some stupid kid?"

He brushed the stray hair from my eyes. "*Non*, because I understand your fear stems from learning far too young that what you love most can be gone in an instant. It is part of what I meant when I said to worry is to love someone. But never doubt that all that I am is yours, and yours alone."

His words overwhelmed me. I wanted to say something meaningful, but nothing came to mind.

Arsène solved my dilemma by placing a chaste kiss on my lips. "We will be fine, *mon amour*. This is only the beginning of our journey. Trust that my love for you is infinite and unshakable, despite it being a new bond between us. It grows deeper every second we spend together, and even more when we are apart and I am missing you."

"You know, there is one upside to a long-distance relationship."

"It makes our reunion that much sweeter?"

"Okay, two benefits." I glanced around to make certain nobody but us would hear what I said next. "We can have sexy fun with video chats."

He lowered his voice, sending a shiver through me. "Are you suggesting we watch each other self-pleasure?"

My dick stirred at the tempting thought. "While I talk dirty to you and you get all domineering with me? Hell yeah."

He officially upgraded me to a semi when he rumbled, "What a naughty little minx you are."

"I told you I had a vivid imagination."

"*Oui*, for which I am most grateful." He took me by the hand. "Come, there is still much to see here."

"Translation: stop being a pervert before I give you a very inconvenient boner?"

He chuckled as he led me away from the fountain. "You are quite gifted at reading between the lines."

"Fine, fine. I'll behave myself for now." Later was a different story, though. If I only had one more night for him to worship me, I intended to savor every moment once we were alone again in the privacy of our bedroom.

As I packed my things at the hotel, the roller coaster of emotions I had been riding on all day due to leaving in the morning hit a major low. I tried not to pout over how upset I was at having to leave Arsène, but it was hard not to throw a tantrum.

"Is there anything I can do to help?" he asked, looking at me with concern.

"Unless you're capable of shrinking yourself down to fit in my suitcase, no." I continued wrapping my souvenirs in my clothing as I put them in my bag. "And I'm pretty sure given who you are, you only fly first class, so that wouldn't work, even if you could contort yourself."

He leaned back against the headboard as he watched

me. "I would much rather upgrade us both if it came down to that. Speaking of which, have you checked in for your flight yet?"

I glanced up at him in confusion for the sudden topic change. "Yeah. Why?"

"Did you not double-check your seat assignment?"

I had been so disgruntled about having to check in that I had hurried through the process without paying much attention. "No?"

"Perhaps you should confirm it now."

His expression gave away nothing, so I took my phone out of my pocket to look. When I pulled up my reservation, my jaw dropped when I saw that I was seat 3A for both legs of my trip home. That was a far cry from the middle seat in the back of the plane I had flown over in. "What the hell? Since when?"

"Since I called your brother while you were asleep and asked him if he would allow me to upgrade your flight. I cannot return with you tomorrow, but I can at least do my small part to take care of you during your journey home."

My eyes started misting up that he would do such a thing for me. Swallowing the lump in my throat, I fought against being overwhelmed by his gesture. "That's not a small part; it's one of the most generous things anyone's ever done for me. Thank you, Arsène. I'd hug you for this, but I'm not sure I could do that right now without sobbing." The fond look he gave me in return almost shattered me. I stared up at the ceiling as I held back tears. "Shit, I'm really going to cry at this rate."

He came over and gathered me into a tight embrace. A sob broke free from me as I clung to him, hiding my face against his strong chest. He stroked my hair to comfort me. "It is fine if you do."

"But I don't want to cry," I whispered, struggling not to be an emotional wreck in front of him. "There's nothing sexy about giving myself a case of the sniffles and puffy eyes."

"You would still be beautiful to me."

How was I supposed to walk away from a man who held me and told me things like that? Tears fell down my cheeks despite my best efforts. "If you thought being a flirt would stop me from weeping, I've got news for you, buddy."

Arsène kissed one of my tears as it fell. The tenderness tore me apart when part of me expected it would be our last goodbye. "*Je t'aime*, Felix. Tears and all."

Shoving at his chest, I complained, "Damn it, I told you to stop being so awesome. Otherwise, they'll have to pry me off you with a crowbar at the airport."

He chuckled before pressing a gentle kiss against my forehead. "*Pardon.* I am not trying to make this harder for you." He wiped away another tear before it could fall. "I will be with you as soon as possible. It is agony having to separate from you."

"I'm not real fond of the packing part, either."

"The sooner you finish, the sooner I can worship every centimeter of you."

I grinned at that. "Now *there's* some incentive I can get behind." Wiping away the tear streaks from my cheeks, I gestured for him to step back. "Fine, let me get my shit together, both literally and figuratively."

Returning to sit at the head of the bed, Arsène kept me laughing as I finished packing the rest of my things. I turned the tables on him by stripping to pack my clothes. Lust burned in his golden gaze as he devoured the sight of me in all my scrawny glory.

It emboldened me to crawl over him on all fours, which caused a visible tenting in his pants as he waited to see what I would do next. I leaned forward and starting trailing kisses up his neck to his ear, tugging on his lobe before murmuring, "I'm ready for the worshipping part to begin."

He roughly flipped me over to pin me underneath him, causing me to whimper at how hot it was that he could take control of me.

Smothering my desire to beg him to fuck me hard, I went for a more playful route instead. "You, sir, are wearing far too many clothes for my tastes."

"And you, monsieur, should have thought about that before pouncing on me." He moved off me to stand beside the bed. I expected him to tear everything off and get right back on top of me, but the goddamn flirt tortured me by doing a sensuous striptease. He peeled off his shirt, revealing one tempting inch of skin at a time, before casting it aside. With a sexy sway of his hips, he moved to the rhythm of an unheard song as he put on a show of stripping out of his jeans.

As I watched him caress his own ass over his black

briefs, I touched myself for some relief. He smirked when he glanced over his shoulder and caught me.

If he thought that would be enough to stop me, he was sorely mistaken. "What?"

"I did not give you permission to touch yourself."

Running my hand up my chest, I tweaked one of my nipples with a breathy noise as I held his gaze. "Are you planning on stopping me?"

"No, but perhaps a punishment is necessary for you being so naughty."

"Uh-uh, you're not allowed to punish me when you're supposed to be worshipping me," I reminded him. "On with the show."

I kept working my cock as he slid his underwear off his magnificent ass, before he turned around to show off his impressive hardness trapped beneath the fabric. Unable to resist, I catcalled, "Take it off, gorgeous. Show me what you've got."

With great flourish, he did a grand reveal as his erection sprang free as he let his briefs drop to the floor. Wrapping his hand around his length, he stroked himself twice to flaunt what a magnificently blessed bastard he was. "Does this meet with your approval?"

"Almost."

He cocked an eyebrow at me, which was so sexy I had to quit touching myself. "And what complaint do you have?"

"It's not inside me."

Arsène kissed me so hard that the room felt like it was spinning from how turned on I was. I arched up to rub my hardness against him with a needy noise that earned me a delicious growl as he sucked on my lower lip.

"*Mon dieu,* you are making it difficult to lovingly worship you when everything you are doing makes me want to ravish you."

"Well, if I get a vote in this, I say fucking ravage me."

He seemed surprised by my response. "Really?"

I slid my hand over his broad shoulders, loving how his muscles bunched under my touch. "Yep, because if you get all reverent and treasure me like the gift I am, I'm going to end up crying because it really will feel like goodbye. If you go all caveman and fuck me hard enough to make me remember I'm yours even after I'm home, I'll feel a lot better."

"That is what you said in the gardens earlier, too."

"I meant it then, and I mean it now," I told him. "Although, if I can put in one request: if you leave a hickey, please don't do it where my brother will see it. He'll flip out, and I'd rather not deal with that."

A dark fire burned in Arsène's golden eyes, making my dick twitch. "You wish for me to mark you?"

As someone who aspired to write romance novels and read a shit ton of them, his question was both sexy and *hilarious*. I burst into peals of laughter that confused him. "Not to ruin the moment, but when you say it that way, you sound like a shifter who is ready to mark me and claim me as a mate!"

"I do not know of what you speak, but I absolutely claim you as mine, now and forever, mark or no mark."

"Of all the romance I could have hoped to experience

in Paris, paranormal was not the one I expected," I said, still laughing. He seemed lost, and I cursed myself for letting my amusement get the best of me. "Okay, okay. Sorry, I didn't mean to wreck the moment. I promise I'll explain it later when you aren't naked, hard, and on top of me. The important thing is that I'm totally down for you to do that, because it's sexy as fuck when all I want is to be yours."

"You are mine," he growled, doing nothing to lessen my amusement over him sounding like a shifter in heat about to claim me as his mate. He refocused my attention with a demanding kiss, making me moan into it from how good it felt to be claimed. His fingers gripped me with a possessiveness that drove me wild as he nipped at my skin and let his scruff brush against me. He was going for broke with dominating me, and I was *living* for it. I was practically mewling as I writhed under him, confident that I'd be returning home with several marks.

By the time he proceeded to giving me a blow job, I gained a whole new appreciation for his talented mouth. As he worked me open with lubed fingers, he drank me all the way to the base like it was nothing. He sucked my dick for everything it was worth, not stopping until I shouted his name as I came.

He swallowed my release, wiping the corner of his lips with his thumb as he looked up at me with a feral expression. I would have come again if it had been possible.

Instead, I cried out with lust as he pushed into me and started a fast and hard pace that felt so good I could barely breathe. Having his fingertips digging into my hips as he drilled me into the mattress had me raking my nails down his back. It was primal passion, and I couldn't get enough of it.

Everything about it was perfect, especially since I would still feel it tomorrow and the day after that at the very least. I wanted the moment to last forever, because as long as I was his, I was happy.

Chapter 12

Arsène

WE BOTH WERE QUIET as I held Felix in bed. I knew he was not asleep yet because he kept petting my facial hair like I was a cat. Lost in my thoughts, I found it strange how my plan to cherish him had fallen apart as my desperation took control of my actions. I had never burned with the need to possess anyone the way I wished to keep him for myself. In four short days, he had changed everything forever. Most shocking of all was I had no complaints or regrets about upending my life if we could be together.

"Can I ask an immature question?"

Pulled from my musings, I focused my attention on the beautiful man in my arms. "Of course."

It took him a moment to build up courage. "What am I allowed to call you?"

"Do you mean like a pet name?"

"No, although we're going to come back to that later, because it's *super* hard to moan 'Arsène' in the middle of sexy times." He continued drawing aimless designs on my skin. "I meant more can I refer to you as my boyfriend when I talk to people?"

I did not understand why that was a question. "You ask that as if you expect me to deny you. Why?"

Felix shrugged. "My last ex hated labels. We fucking lived together, but he got hives if I called him my boyfriend. And I wondered why he cheated on me, ugh."

I hugged him tighter as I kissed his forehead. "Yet another reason to despise him. I have no such hang-ups."

"What about you? Would you ever refer to me that way?" The insecurity in his voice pained me. "I mean, I get that it's probably embarrassing for you to date someone so much younger than you, but—"

"Nothing about you embarrasses me, nor am I ashamed of our age gap. I am honored to call you my boyfriend."

He shifted to look up at me with guarded hope. "Really?"

"I would never lie to you. There is nothing shameful about falling for somebody as remarkable as you. Please believe me."

"Damn it, you're going to make me cry again." His eyes grew glassy with tears.

"In that case, I will save my pep talk about believing in your abilities for another time. Perhaps when you need encouragement to write your first book."

He sat up to face me. "Wait, you're serious? For all you know, I could be a shitty writer."

I chuckled at the ridiculous notion. "You have a way with words that paint colorful pictures. Combined with your vividly naughty imagination, I am confident that you are a gifted author. I wish to see you pursue whatever makes you happy. I believe writing does that for you, *non*?"

"Well, yeah, when I'm not wishing to throw my computer out a window and scream into the void because nothing is coming out how I want it to."

Running my fingers through his soft hair, I asked, "You write romantic fairy tales, right?"

"I try to, but they always ring hollow, especially when I read North's stuff. He's so much further ahead of me, even though we're the same age. In fairness, he has more experience than me, but—"

I shushed his criticism. "One thing I have learned in my career is comparison is the thief of joy. You cannot compare the start of your journey to his middle. That only brings frustration."

"Wow, that's fucking deep." He laughed as he gazed at me with wonder. "But how do I know how I'm doing if I don't measure myself against other people?"

"Judge where you are by where you want to be, not by where others are."

He gave an impressed whistle. "Damn, I never realized sage advice was a benefit of dating an older man. I should start taking notes. It's like I've enrolled in an advanced philosophy class with the hottest professor ever."

I chuckled over his response. "I will say one more thing in that case."

He pretended to write on his hand. "Okay, I'm ready. Lay it on me."

"Perhaps you were unsatisfied with the romance you wrote because your own life experience was lacking in that regard."

"You're suggesting since you've shown me what true love is, I'll be able to tell more authentic stories?" He tapped his lip as he mulled over the idea.

"I believe you could do it before, but perhaps now you will have the confidence to trust in your writer's instinct."

He leaned in to give me a sweet kiss. "God, dating you keeps getting better and better. That's one hell of a perk, I've gotta say."

"I look forward to seeing what stories I can inspire."

He flashed a cheeky grin. "Good, because you're going to *love* the research stage when I ask you to help me figure out if certain positions are possible."

"I am always happy to volunteer my services as your assistant. However, it is getting late. You should try to rest. Tomorrow will be a long day."

His pout was adorable. "But if I go to sleep, it'll be morning too soon."

"I know, but you must."

His lingering kiss made me wish things were different. "Only because I have to, not because I want to." He shut off the bedside lamp before snuggling against me once more, sprawling out as he draped his arm and leg over me. "Thanks for giving me the vacation of a lifetime."

"I am the one who should be saying *merci beaucoup* for making me the happiest I've ever been. *Je t'aime, mon amour.*"

"Damn, maybe you should try your hand at romance novels, too. You'd be as amazing at it as you are at everything else." Kissing my chest, he nuzzled against me with a contented sigh. "Love you."

As he drifted to sleep, I continued holding him in the dark, savoring his nearness. It would have to be enough to get me through our lonely nights apart.

Before Felix's arrival, I had expected to be counting down the days until I dropped him off at the airport. I had been confident that I would be more than ready for my life to return to normal and never spend another moment thinking about my younger brother's friend.

Oh, how wrong I had been. It was sheer agony knowing I would have to stand there and watch him walk away from me. It took a shameful amount of willpower not to book a ticket to return to Sunnyside with him. Even if our time apart would be brief, it was the worst kind of hell. Ripping my heart out of my chest would have hurt less. How could I let him leave me when everything inside me was begging to hold on to him forever?

If I had not yet been convinced of my love for Felix, his imminent departure made it undeniable. Regardless of the fact we had only spent five days together, it felt like I was losing the other half of my soul. I did my best to put on a brave face so it would not be harder on him than it had to be, but it was difficult.

After he checked in his luggage, seeing him standing next to his roller carry-on tore me to shreds knowing he was about to leave.

"Okay, I swear to god I'm going to get through this without crying," he declared with adorable determination. "The last thing I want is your final mental picture of me to be with red eyes and sniffling snot. That means no romantic declarations out of you, got it?"

I held up my hands in surrender. "You have my word."

He threw his arms around me in a bear hug, burying his face against my neck. I smiled when he inhaled deeply. "Fuck, I should have stolen a bottle of your cologne as a souvenir. I wasn't thinking."

"Would you spray your pillow with it to keep you company at night so it was almost like I was with you?"

"Yeah, let's go with that and pretend I'm not a pervert who would get off on your scent."

I laughed at how unrepentant he was about such a thing. "Ah, that is a shame. If it was the latter, you could have persuaded me to send you a bottle in the mail."

"Would a promise of using it to put on a solo show for you during our video call change your mind?"

It was difficult not to moan at the fantasy of him pleasuring himself while getting off to the smell of me. "If I am not allowed to make any romantic declarations, you cannot torture me with perverse ones."

His ornery grin was too much. "It's probably for the best. I don't want to go through security with a hard-on. It might get a little awkward when they ask what I'm trying to smuggle through Customs in my pants."

"*Oui*, that pleasure is for me, and me alone."

"Well, you and my right hand," he retorted with a

wink as he stepped back. "If you're good, I'll let you watch."

It took an effort not to kiss him in retaliation. "I shall look forward to that once you are home and settled."

"You and me both." A little of the playfulness left his expression as he turned serious. "I can't ever thank you enough for what you've done for me. This vacation has been a dream come true."

I cradled his cheek in my palm. "Since I am forbidden from making any grand proclamations of my feelings for you, I shall simply say that I am thankful for the time we could spend together. I will be glad once we reunite and do not have to part anymore."

"Admit it. You were totally expecting to hate me before I arrived. I bet you thought I was going to be an annoying American kid you couldn't wait to get rid of."

"I had hoped my brother had better taste in friends than that. Thankfully, I am thrilled with how things turned out, though," I told him. "My only regret is your trip was not longer."

"Same. But I spent all of my savings since high school on this adventure. Even then, I couldn't have pulled it off without Augie and Brody's help."

It was comforting to know he had support. "I am grateful their assistance allowed you to come here. It is wonderful that you have that kind of relationship with your brother's boyfriend."

"Yeah, Brody is the best," Felix said with a fond smile. "He snuck me extra Euros and made me promise to use them on myself, since he knew the rest of my cash was going toward gifts for everyone. I don't think he told Augie, because my brother would have given me a lecture about spending money frivolously."

"You are loved by many."

"I'm definitely lucky," he agreed. "Especially now that I get to include you on the list of people who adore me."

I was the fortunate one. "That makes me the happiest of all."

He gave me a warning look. "Hey, you're getting dangerously close to being romantic, monsieur."

"*Pardon*. It is surprisingly difficult not to profess my great love and affection for you."

"Okay, then I need to hurry up and go before you make me weep like a lady next to a rainy window after reading a letter from her beloved on the war front."

I chuckled despite my sadness. "What an unusually specific description."

"Yeah, I'm prone to dramatics sometimes. My brother always jokes I missed my calling as an actor." His good humor faded once more, replaced by tumultuous emotions that begged me to hold him and never let go. "I refuse to tell you goodbye because that's too final. You can't say it, either."

"Perhaps a promise to see you soon would be best?"

He nodded. "I can live with that. Is it okay if I video call you once I'm home after my brother lets me out of his sight?"

"Please do. Even if it is late or early, that is fine."

"I'll text you when I land at both airports before that, unless that's too clingy for you," he said with concern.

Brushing my thumb over the worried furrow of his brow, I reassured him, "It would comfort me to know you have arrived. Please message me whenever you would like. If you ever wonder if I wish to hear from you, the answer is always yes."

He exhaled a sigh of relief. "Okay, that's good. I don't want to annoy you long-distance."

"The only way you could do that is if you do not contact me because you are afraid of being a nuisance."

Felix hugged me once more, and I held him tight. "I have to leave now, because I'm about to lose my battle to keep my cool." He looked up at me with teary eyes. "Thank you, I love you, and I'll see you soon, okay?"

I kissed him with need, not ready to let him go, even though I must. "You are welcome, *je t'aime*, and I cannot wait until you are in my arms once more, *mon amour*." There was so much more to say, but I left it at that for both of our sakes.

My heart shattered the moment he left my embrace. I stayed where I was until he reached security, laughing when the little minx blew me a kiss before waving goodbye and disappearing from my sight.

When I returned to my apartment without Felix, the hole in my heart ached with his absence. To distract myself,

I sat down to go through the pictures I had taken of him. I started with the ones from our tours of the famous landmarks. The sight of his happy smile brought one to my face.

It was the first time I had viewed the photo shoot we had done downstairs in my studio. I fell in love with him all over again as I clicked through them all. The shots of him in the chair had come out better than I had hoped. I could have won awards with the photograph of his impish smirk from when he had been teasing me.

I saved the photo shoot in my bedroom after our first time together for last. The sight of him in sensuous repose made my prick throb with need and my heart break anew at losing him. I paused on an image of him that took my breath away. There was nothing more beautiful to me in the entire world than seeing his adoration shining up at me with his smile.

"That's why you're leaving, isn't it?"

I spun my chair around at the sound of Armand's voice coming from behind me. It surprised me that instead of his normal, arrogant teasing, he looked at me with the understanding only a childhood best friend could have. "What do you mean?"

He gestured at the photo on my screen. "When he looks at you with such love, how could you not follow him to the ends of the earth?"

I rubbed my chest over my heart, which physically pained me from my loss. "Will you try to talk me out of it?"

"Honestly, I'm shocked you're here and not on the

plane with him." He crossed his arms over his chest as he leaned against the doorframe and studied me.

That wasn't the answer I had expected. "I suppose you think I have lost my mind for wanting to follow him to America?"

"As long as I have known you, you've let nothing stop you from getting what you want. Why should he be any different?"

He was right. "Do you believe I am making a mistake?"

"In staying here instead of going back with him?"

I shook my head. "Setting up a new studio in Sunnyside for the sake of being near him."

"*Non*, which is why I'll help you on both sides of the ocean. Perhaps I can find an American cutie of my own while I'm out there with you. He must have some sexy single friends who would swoon for my French accent."

I experienced a rush of fondness for my oldest and closest friend. "For that, I will forgive you for how you woke him up the other morning."

"My offer for a threesome still stands."

Once again, my primal urge to protect Felix stirred within me, even though I knew he wasn't in real danger. "I think you say that only because you enjoy having me shoot you down."

"Hey, you can't blame a guy for trying when he's that cute. Your poor heart never stood a chance."

"Not at all."

"We have a few things we need to take care of before

you catch your flight tomorrow to return to your new beau."

I arched an eyebrow at him. "What makes you so certain I will do such a thing?"

He reached behind him and pulled out a plane ticket from the rear pocket of his jeans. "Because your best friend in the world has already made the arrangements for you. You'll be there by ten o'clock at night, just in time to kiss your beloved good night. I also set up an appointment for you with Rune's Realtor the next afternoon so you can sleep in, because I'm thoughtful like that."

I got up to hug Armand, the tightness in my chest lessening, knowing I'd be seeing Felix sooner than I had expected. *"Merci, mon ami."*

He clasped my shoulder and gave it a squeeze. "I'm happy for you. His bright spark is the light you need. Your photographs already show the difference love has made in your life in such a short time."

"That it has. Come, let us get to work. There is much to do before I leave." I could not wait until I could surprise Felix and hold him in my arms again soon.

Chapter 13

Felix

As I entered the baggage claim area, it wasn't hard to miss my brother and his boyfriend waiting for me in the airport. Tall, jacked, and handsome as hell, Brody stuck out amongst the crowd. With his red hair and wearing a black T-shirt that showed off his ridiculously muscular arms, he was an imposing figure, which was hilarious considering how nice he was. He looked like a bouncer, dwarfing my worrywart brother's smaller frame, who wore a teal button-down shirt, pink undershirt, and jeans.

The instant I was within touching range, my brother embraced me so tightly that breathing became a challenge. He hugged me like I had been gone for five years and not five days. Despite hating leaving Arsène behind in Paris, it was good to reunite with Augie.

"Thank god you're home safe," he told me, still refusing to let go. "I'm sorry I worried so much, but—"

"It's okay. With my track record, I don't blame you for fearing I might start an international incident." I knew he always felt guilty about his anxiety, so I did my best to not make it worse for him.

He pulled back to look at me. "It's not that I don't trust you. There are so many things out there that could hurt you, and when I'm so far away—" Augie's voice cracked at the thought of harm befalling me when he couldn't help me. "Sorry, I tried to be okay with everything, but I didn't do a very good job."

"You let me go and didn't show up on a spontaneous 'vacation' to check up on me in person. That's huge."

He frowned, frustrated with himself over his reaction to me being gone. "The last thing I want is for you to resent me because I'm not treating you like an adult."

"I promise I'm not mad. You didn't forbid me from going. And even if I was here and told you I'd call you and didn't, you would have called whoever I was with to make sure I was fine. Please don't feel bad. Just be happy I'm home, okay? Because it was super tempting to stay for longer."

Augie gave me another hug before releasing me. "Oh, I definitely am. I hope you had fun over there."

"I'm quite certain that he did," Brody said, before taking his turn greeting me. He lowered his voice so only I would hear him. "I'm sure a lot of it was the naked sexy kind, too."

I laughed as I squeezed him tighter. It was like embracing a brick wall of muscles because he was so built, but he gave some of the best hugs in the world. As a reformed playboy devoted to my older brother, he knew what antics I had gotten up to with Arsène. "Can you blame me?"

He patted my shoulder with a fond look when he stepped back. "Not one damn bit. Good for you, lad. I'm proud of you." He grabbed my luggage off the carousel and started ushering us to leave.

Augie at least had the decency to wait until we were in the car to ask, "So, are we going to talk about Arsène?"

I kept my voice neutral. "What about him?"

He turned to look at me from the front passenger seat as Brody drove. "Is he in love with you?"

I tried to play dumb. "Is this because he upgraded me to first class?" Leaving him sucked, but doing it in style had been awesome.

"He's going to break your heart, Felix, if he hasn't already."

"I can promise you, my heart is still very much in one piece," I assured him. It was no small miracle, either.

He narrowed his eyes. "Are you telling me you didn't fall for him?"

"Maybe we should get dinner first before you give him the third-degree interrogation?" Brody suggested.

While I appreciated the out, I figured it would be better to throw it all out there. "Yes, I love him. No, I'm not heartbroken about it, because against all odds, it's not one-sided."

Augie's expression turned pitying. "He seems nice, but long distance is—"

"Not going to be a problem for us, because it's only temporary." I said a silent prayer that Arsène wouldn't make me a liar. "He's planning on relocating here to set up a second studio soon." I neglected to mention that had anything to do with me. I didn't want to freak out my older brother about us moving too fast.

"But—"

Brody reached over and caressed the back of his

boyfriend's head to soothe him. "I know you're looking for problems so you can fix them. But let's celebrate he fell in love with a good man who treats him right. After that last arsehole ex of his, Felix deserves the happiness we have. If it comes in the form of a gorgeous, rich, sexy Frenchman spoiling him, all the better."

Augie sighed. "I'm sorry, you're right. He seems like a nice guy. And he gets bonus points for not getting annoyed with me for calling him so late when I checked on you."

"He's an older brother, too, so he understands," I said. "He told me worrying is how you show you love me."

"Probably the most annoying way."

I grinned back at him. "God only knows what kind of trouble I'd get into if I didn't worry about your reactions."

"I'd rather not think about that, thanks."

"Try to think of where we should have dinner instead," Brody told us.

As we debated our options, I pulled out my phone to send Arsène a quick text my family had picked me up at the airport. It was after two in the morning in Paris, so it surprised me when I got a response.

Arsène: *I am glad you will be home soon.*

Felix: *Not too soon. We're getting dinner first, then I'm sure I'll talk to North once I'm back at our apartment. By the time I can video chat with you, it'll be at least 7:00 a.m. in Paris.*

Arsène: *In that case, I will get some sleep so I may wake up to enjoy that.*

It was hard to smother my grin so as not to tip off my brother.

Felix: *Did you stay up late to hear from me?*

Arsène: *Oui, I could not rest until I knew you were safe.*

Felix: *Damn, that's pretty romantic of you.*

Arsène: *So was editing the pictures I took of you, so I could spend today with you and your smiling face.*

It was impossible not to swoon. The sweet sentiment also had potential for some naughtiness I couldn't help but tease him with. If he stayed up late for my sake, I could at least give him some entertainment.

Felix: *Are you trying to make me cry long-distance or give me a hard-on? Because the answer depends on if you were wistfully looking at the Versailles ones or getting off to the bedroom shoot.*

Arsène: *Do you wish for me to regale you with a*

tale of how I pleasured myself while enjoying looking at a picture of you in my bed?

Oh, if he wanted to play, it was game on. I typed back a flirty response.

Felix: *My cock is super into that. Too bad I'm in the back seat of Brody's car and can't take proper advantage of sexting right now.*

"How does that sound, Felix?"

I startled at my brother saying my name. "Huh?"

Brody smirked at my distraction. "Are you in the mood for burgers?"

"Oh, that would be great, thanks. Sorry."

He winked at me in the rearview mirror, causing me to bite my lip to hold in a laugh. He obviously knew what I was up to with Arsène. Thank god he was cool enough not to blow my cover. "We're about ten minutes away from the restaurant if you want to give him an update."

Augie chuckled. "I'm sure North would appreciate the heads-up. It's a miracle you haven't walked in on him and Elias yet. It's probably only a matter of time."

Neither of us bothered to correct him about who I was talking to.

My phone vibrated in my hand with another message.

Arsène: *You can still tempt me into naughtiness, even with an ocean between us.*

Felix: *That's rich coming from the man who's tempting me something fierce with the promise of sexting when I can't get off because dinner is in ten minutes.*

Arsène: *It is probably for the best. I wish to watch you do that together with me in the morning.*

Felix: *That makes two of us. I can't wait to see you explode all over your fist and stomach as I imagine you coming inside me instead.*

There was a long delay as the three dots flashed while he took his time typing a response. His inability to come up with an immediate reply amused the hell out of me.

Felix: *Oops, sorry. Was that too much?*

Arsène: *Too much, and not enough. I shall get my revenge later, mon amour. Enjoy your dinner.*

It was fun teasing him, even though I was torturing myself at the same time.

Felix: *I'd much rather have your dick in my mouth than a burger.*

Arsène: *What an impish little minx you are. It is almost like you are begging for me to punish you.*

Felix: *There's only one way to find out if I'm into that kink with you. It's kind of exciting, not gonna lie.*

Arsène: *Then I guess it is a good thing you are determined to be naughty enough to earn a punishment.*

Felix: *Is it bad that kinda makes me want to write back "Fuck me, daddy" when you say that? Because daddy kink isn't my thing, but it seems like the right response.*

Arsène: *It looks as if I will have to get creative in punishing you.*

Felix: *Is it better if I say "Fuck me up real good, baby" instead?*

Once again, the blipping dots appeared for a long time, causing me to push things further. It was too much fun with him.

Felix: *Too bad you can't stick your cock in my mouth to shut me up like you can in person, right?*

Arsène: *Mon dieu. You are too much sometimes.*

Felix: *Oh, please. You and your erection fucking love this.*

Arsène: *Your punishment is I will not share a picture of it.*

Felix: *Damn, I didn't know dick pics were an option.*

Arsène: *Perhaps you should have thought about that before teasing me when you do not have the time for a proper follow-through.*

Felix: *So I guess now's a bad time to announce we're almost at the restaurant?*

Arsène: *Go eat. We will enjoy ourselves soon.*

Felix: *Looking forward to it.*

I hesitated before adding one more thing. It was risky, but I had to say it to see how he responded.

Felix: *Love you.*

Arsène: *As I love you, even when you leave me hard and wanting.*

Felix: *Now who's being the cocktease?*

Arsène: *You inspire it in me.*

Felix: *I'm fine with that being my fault. Sleep well and dream of me. I'll text you when I'm home.*

Arsène: *Bonne nuit, mon amour.*

His words filled me with warm fuzzies. It helped reassure me I hadn't misinterpreted his interest in me or made everything up in my head. I couldn't wait until later, but first was dinner with my family.

It was a relief to return to my apartment after a long meal. I was dead-ass exhausted and ready to drop, but I had to stay awake. There wasn't a chance I was missing out on my video call with Arsène.

North gave me a big hug when I entered. "Welcome back! God, it was way too quiet without you here."

I glanced around, a bit surprised he was alone. "Really? I figured Elias would keep you company while I was gone and Westie would be here trying to ruin your fun."

We went over to sit on the couches in our living room. I melted into the comforts of being home after a long damn day of travel.

"Trust me, she wanted to be here when you got back, but her boss is making her put in overtime with their new

Fall launch coming up." She worked for Kalindi Urslana, the fashion designer who was famous for her gorgeous designs and ridiculously high standards of perfectionism. "That's literally the only thing in the world that would keep her away from her favorite Fifi."

Knowing how tough her boss was, I had extra sympathy for her. "Wow, it must be bad, because she isn't texting me."

"Don't worry, she'll be over here to love all over you as soon as possible. How was dinner with your brother and Brody?"

"It was good! Dad surprised me by meeting us there, which was great," I replied. Since it was only the three of us after losing Mom, we were a tight-knit family. "Paris was fun, but I missed everyone more than I expected."

North was always quick to joke. "I'm amazed Arsène gave you time to miss anyone. I was certain he'd keep you too busy."

I grinned at him. "You know I heard the 'in bed' part even without you saying it, right?"

"Yeah, you lucky bastard. If I wasn't madly in love with Elias, I'd be hella jealous." He laughed as he leaned back on the couch.

I stretched my legs out on the coffee table, savoring the slight soreness in my muscles that lingered from Arsène claiming me. It low-key turned me on, which was probably weird. "Now that I'm home, it almost feels like it was all a dream."

"I'm sure he gave you enough of a workout to remind your body it really happened," he said, winking at me like the shameless flirt he'd always be. "You don't look heartbroken, so I'm assuming that's a good sign."

"He talked about moving here, but part of me worries it was just the lust talking." I sighed as I crossed my arms over my chest. "I tried not to take it personally that my brother thinks Arsène is out of his mind for wanting to move here after spending only five days together."

"See, that's the great thing about being with an older guy. They know what they want and aren't afraid to do something about it."

I snickered at that. "You say that like Elias is fourteen years older than you and not four."

"I'm not wrong. I'm glad Arsène is smart enough to not let you go. You're too fucking awesome to not have a man ready to worship you on his knees for all of eternity. Trust me, there were definitely days where I wondered why I was too stupid to try."

I laughed at his declaration. We had joked about it in the past, but we had never been serious. As someone who wanted a relationship, North's refusal to settle down with anyone until he met Elias was incompatible with what I needed. "That's because the thought of commitment made you break out in a rash until you met Elias. For what it's worth, there were nights when I felt like a moron for not taking you up on your flirting, and fucking to get it out of our system."

He groaned. "I'll pretend I didn't hear you say I almost stood a chance with you."

I nudged him with my foot. "Take it as the compliment it's meant to be. You're too good of a friend to lose to fucking. Amongst our friends, no one gets down to my level in the gutter like you do."

"Hell yeah I do, although we both know I'm usually a couple of layers of filth lower than you."

I snorted at that. "Only because my filter occasionally works enough to realize there are certain thoughts I should keep to myself."

"Pfft, filters are overrated," he scoffed. "I'm really happy for you, man. Arsène seems like a pretty cool guy. I won't complain about seeing his handsome face around here all the time."

"Yeah, I bet." Sighing, I shook my head. "I hope he comes here and it wasn't an empty promise."

"He'll be here before you know it."

My exhaustion hit me full force. "Speaking of which, I'm going to talk to him before I crash. I'm fucking beat after traveling all day."

He waved at me. "See you in the afternoon. Enjoy your cute 'No, you hang up' call."

"Try not to listen in."

North's eyes lit up with the potential for perverse fun. "Why? Are you planning on making it sexy?"

His question reminded me to wear headphones and keep my voice down while I chatted with my boyfriend. "Not for your sake."

He laughed at my answer. "Get some rest. We'll have a proper catch-up tomorrow."

After getting ready for bed, I locked the door behind me before texting Arsène.

Felix: *You up?*

It was a little disappointing when he didn't immediately respond, but it was stupid early in France. I killed time looking at social media. After checking my feed, I went back through my own posts to enjoy all of our pictures and videos. It helped to have incontrovertible evidence about our adventure. I rewatched a video of us kissing, which got a rise out of a certain part of me. While I had a momentary debate over if it was weird to touch myself while watching us, Arsène saved me with a text.

Arsène: *Indeed I am.*

Felix: *Are you ready for a naughty call, or would you prefer a normal one?*

Arsène: *I would suspect that a normal one is still quite naughty when you are involved.*

Felix: *You know me so well. In that case, me and my hard dick are very excited to see you.*

Stripping out of my pajamas, I positioned my laptop on a stack of pillows before putting in my wireless earbuds so North wouldn't eavesdrop on our private time. He was loyal to Elias, but I had no doubts he'd get off on us like we were free porn. There was something embarrassing about being so exposed in front of the camera, but my erection had no such shyness.

When Arsène appeared on-screen, he was naked, sitting in his office with his door closed, and his prick standing proudly at full attention. Mine twitched at the sight, appreciating the view.

He was the first to speak. "How good to see I am not the only one who is up."

Hearing his voice in my headphones made him sound closer, sending shivers through me. "What can I say?" I trailed my fingers along the underside of my hardness from base to tip. "I'm up for fun, and down to fuck."

"My marks look exquisite on your skin." He rumbled with pleasure as he brushed over the spots on his side that mirrored the hickeys he gave me.

I mimicked his actions, enjoying the sensation when I pressed against the small love bites. "Yeah, I wish you had left more. I love being claimed by you."

"If I were there, I would give you a dominating kiss that would leave no doubts in your mind that you are mine. Let me hear you," he commanded in a tone of voice that left me with no choice but to obey as precum beaded on my tip.

I tilted my head to the side as I ran my fingers down the curve of my neck and down my chest. "Kiss me all over, Arsène." I traced circles over my nipples before tweaking them into stiff peaks. When he didn't say anything, I spread my thighs wider apart and made a show of spreading my precum over the crown of my dick.

Of course, in true me fashion, I kicked my laptop off its pillow perch in the process. "Oops, sorry."

"Even from this angle, you are lovely."

"Yeah, I'm sure you're really enjoying the close-up of my sexy shinbone," I said with a snort as I put it back on the pillows. Somehow, I managed to disconnect our call while adjusting it. "Oh, goddamn it! Stop cockblocking me, computer! I swear to god, I'll throw you out the window if you keep acting up like this."

I called him back and scowled as he laughed at me. "You seem to be having some technical difficulties."

"In my defense, it's really hard to multitask when everything in me is screaming to get off to the sight of you touching yourself." Being more careful this time, I stretched out to give him the best view without bumping into my makeshift pillow tripod. "Is that good?"

"It is perfect. I only wish I was there so I could fall to my knees and worship every centimeter of you. Never forget that you are mine."

The possessive growl in his voice made me want to push him further. "I want you so much, Arsène."

"Show me."

I wrapped my hand around my length and stroked myself for his enjoyment. "When I think of you touching me, it gets me all hot and bothered."

It was so sexy watching him jerk off that it almost distracted me from what I was trying to do. I arched up and wantonly moaned his name. It was hard not to smirk when he muttered *"Nom de dieu"* under his breath at my performance.

An idea came to mind, so I decided it was worth it to try. Hopefully, he'd think it was sexy and not stupid. "I want to suck your dick so bad," I groaned, earning me an interesting rumble from him. I put on an elaborate display of sucking on two of my fingers like I was giving a blow job. His hand picked up speed at the sight, so I kept it up, getting them nice and wet before pulling them out of my mouth.

Not content to stop there, I teased my hole with my slicked fingers. "Fuck, I need you and your massive dick filling me up inside."

"There is nothing I want more than to be buried in your tight heat." He reached down with his other hand to tease his sac. "I will not be satisfied until I have come inside you once more."

"Fuck yeah, it's so sexy feeling your hot cum inside me, marking me as yours."

Even with the screens and oceans separating us, the heat of his gaze burned me up with lust. "The sight of me leaking out of you—" He moaned at the thought. "It makes me wish to lick you clean and go again."

Imagining him rimming me pushed me to my edge. "Shit, I'm so close. Just a little more, *please!*" I was too far gone to care about how desperate I sounded.

He played dirty by growling something sexy in French. I barely had enough time to cover my mouth to hold in my muffled cry as I shot my load onto my stomach. For my sanity, I'd pretend that North probably hadn't heard me.

It was euphoric watching Arsène come with my name on his lips, milking his cock until it was spent.

Lowering my hand, I trembled from my release. "Damn, that was way sexier than I expected."

"Your wicked mouth can undo me every time," he said with a rueful shake of his head. "You have not been gone twenty-four hours and I am already bereft without you."

"That makes me feel less bad about how much I miss you," I admitted. "Sleeping alone again is going to suck."

"I can confirm that is a fact. My bed was too lonely without you there in my arms last night."

A dreamy sigh escaped from me without my permission. "You're so good at being romantic. I really should start taking notes."

He reached off-screen for a tissue to clean himself, reminding me to do the same. "Are you planning to study me later?"

"Yeah, kinda." I tossed my dirty tissue but missed the trash can by a country mile. "I don't know if that will weird you out, though."

"Forgive me, but I seem to be too lost in the afterglow to follow what you mean."

Considering what we had just done, it was silly to get shy now. "Um, well, the thing is, you really inspired me. I started a new book on the flight home."

He brightened with excitement for me. "That is wonderful to hear! What is it about?"

"Prince Leander Montarelli falls in love with a sassy librarian named Cyrus Valan, who gives him hell in the royal library." I bit my lower lip as I waited for his reaction. "I'm thinking of calling it *The Prince and His Librarian*, because all good fairy tales have titles like that. I don't know, it's probably a cheesy idea, but—"

He refused to let me finish protesting. "*Non*, I think it sounds *très magnifique*, Felix. This is exciting news!"

His response gave me hope. "The characters aren't based on us per se, but there might be enough similarities that it makes you uncomfortable. I mean, the prince *is* pretty awesome, with emphasis on the pretty, of course."

"What if we make a deal, eh? You can borrow elements of me for a character if I can exhibit some photos of you in my next show."

His offer thrilled me, but I hesitated to accept. "I don't know if that's a fair trade. Even if I finish the book, nobody will read it other than my friends. The entire fashion world would care about your exhibition, though."

"I have no doubts that your debut novel will be a bestseller," he said with a confidence I wished I possessed.

"Yeah, right. Bestseller is way too high of a goal to aim for with my first book."

He refused to let it go. "I am so sure of your success, I will provide your cover photo with my name attached."

My jaw dropped at his offer. "Wow, that's beyond generous of you, but maybe you should read my work first before agreeing to associate your name with mine. I'd hate to embarrass you."

"I will be happy to read your story. But I am sure my offer will still stand."

The show of support touched me, although I thought

he was foolish for offering. "God, I want to hug you so much for that. Ugh, oceans suck."

He chuckled at my pouting. "They do. You should rest. It has been a very long day for you."

"I'll text you later?"

"Please do. Forgive me if I am a little slow in responding today," he said. "I have quite a few meetings that will tie up my schedule, so I am sorry about that. I promise I will make it up to you tonight."

"You better." I ached to curl up at his side and fall asleep in his arms again. "I love you. Thank you again for everything. First class was awesome. You've spoiled me forever."

"And I will continue to do so. *Je t'aime, mon amour. Bonne nuit.*"

After ending the call, I had enough energy left to turn off my lamp and put my laptop on my nightstand before passing the fuck out into a deep sleep.

Chapter 14

Arsène

By the time I arrived at Felix's apartment, I was beyond exhausted after a long day of travel. It was almost midnight, but he had not replied to any of my recent texts. Thankfully, my younger brother had provided me with the address, or my surprise would have been off to a disastrous start.

I knocked on the door, but Felix was not the one who answered. A young man stared at me in shocked awe, wearing rainbow-colored pajama pants and a purple T-shirt. He was cute, with blue-green eyes and wavy blond hair. I wondered if I had the wrong apartment until he exclaimed, "Holy shit, you're fucking *gorgeous!*"

Having heard many stories about Felix's roommate and his lack of a filter, it was easy to guess who was standing in front of me. "*Bonsoir*. You must be North."

His lopsided grin was roguish. "So my reputation precedes me, huh? Damn, it's not fair you're even more attractive in person than in pictures." He stepped aside and gestured for me to enter. "Sorry, come in."

"*Merci*." I glanced around the comfortable living room but saw no one else. "Where is Felix?"

"Jet lag has been kicking his ass today, so he went to bed early. He didn't mention you stopping by, which is weird, since that seems like something he would've been shouting from the rooftops."

"That is because he did not know I was coming," I explained. "I wished to surprise him. It seems there have been several flaws in my plan so far."

"He's definitely going to be shocked." North chuckled as he pointed down the hall. "His bedroom is there if you want to wake him up and give him the good news."

I gestured to my luggage. "Would you mind if I leave this in the living room? I would hate to disturb him by taking this in there."

"Sure, that's fine with me. Let me see if Elias is up for a late-night visit from me so you can have the place to yourselves tomorrow."

"That is very kind of you, but I do not wish to banish you from your own home."

North pulled his phone out of his pocket to message his boyfriend. A response came immediately. "You're in luck. He wants me to stay with him, so my night just got a lot better, thanks." He winked at me. "Have fun in the morning without worrying about me. Text me when the coast is clear."

"Felix is right. You are a good roommate and friend."

He grinned at that. "Sure, until I forget to do the dishes. Anyway, it was nice meeting you and your handsome face, Arsène. I'll see you tomorrow after you two have had a chance to get reacquainted."

With another word of thanks, I used the toilet before I entered Felix's room. I could not make out much detail in the dark, but I saw him illuminated by the hallway light, facing away from me. I shut the door, then stripped out of my clothes. As gingerly as possible, I eased myself into bed with him, doing my best not to disturb his slumber. He didn't stir as I curled up behind him, but he murmured in his sleep as I molded myself around him in an embrace. The tension left my body as I relaxed against him, my exhaustion hitting me hard. Even though I was in a place I had never been before, it still felt like coming home because Felix was in my arms once more.

I AWOKE TO THE sound of a startled cry and a loud *thud*. Blinking in confusion, I saw Felix on the ground, staring up at me with his mouth agape in the gray light of early dawn. "Why are you on the floor, *mon amour*?"

He did not move from where he sat. "Why the hell are you in my bed?"

"Because I came here last night to surprise you, but you were already asleep," I explained. "That does not explain why you are down there, though."

"Fucking hell, I thought you were a stranger who broke into my apartment, and I panicked." He sighed in relief before he straddled over me.

Felix caught me off guard when he pinched my side hard enough to cause me to jerk in surprise. "Ow! What was that for?"

"To make sure you were real."

Scowling, I rubbed my sore spot. "When you are

checking if you are dreaming, you are supposed to see if *you* feel pain, not me."

"It definitely hurt when my bony ass hit the floor. I hope you enjoy laughing at that bruise later." He grinned, looking extra boyish with his hair sticking up at odd angles from sleep. "Sorry, I had to be sure you were real and not the best dream ever."

"I assure you I am here."

He did a poor job of stifling a yawn. "Um, I hate to ruin your wonderful gesture by being all, 'Wow, that's *so* romantic that you flew all the way over here to surprise me! Can I go back to bed now?' But I'm *exhausted*, and it's too early to be conscious."

I chuckled as I wrapped my arms around him in a loose embrace. "Do not feel badly. I am still tired after my long trip, so I have no complaints about getting more rest."

"God, you really are the best." He placed a sweet, lingering kiss on my lips before curling up on me with a sleepy murmur. "I promise I'll make it up to you when we wake up later."

"North volunteered to stay with Elias until we text him that he is free to return, so we will have plenty of time and privacy to get reacquainted."

"That's awesome," Felix said through a yawn. "Love you. G'night."

I hugged him and pressed a soft kiss on his forehead. The weight of him on my chest was reassuring as I held him. I had everything I wanted in life, right there in my arms.

Hours later, I woke up with Felix curled against my side as I faced him. The very nearness of him set my soul at ease. As I gazed at his beautiful face, it made me want to grab my camera. However, I could not bear to leave his side for even a moment, nor did I wish to disturb him.

It was difficult to resist reaching out to touch him. Instead, I studied the curve of his long eyelashes, the gentle slope of the bridge of his nose, and the soft edges of his delicate cheekbones. His full lips begged for me to cover them with my own.

"If you're not here, I'm going to be *so* pissed at you," he mumbled before peeking with one eye to check if I was there. Both of his eyes flew open in shock when he saw me smiling at him. That close, I could see the flecks of gold in his jade green that gave them such depth. He reached out to caress my cheek with trembling fingers as he breathed in awe, "Oh, thank god. It wasn't just a dream."

When I leaned closer to kiss him, he rebuffed me by putting his hand up to stop my lips from claiming his. I kissed his fingertips instead, making him giggle. "Is there some reason you are stopping me from kissing you?"

"Yes, because kissing leads to sexy things."

"And the problem with that is what?"

He gave me a sheepish look. "Sorry, but I *really* have to pee first." I laughed hard as he scrambled away from me to make a beeline for the exit. "It's not funny! I've been asleep for like twelve hours without taking a piss!

Excuse me for wanting to use the bathroom before my stupid dick makes aiming impossible."

I continued laughing as he rushed to the toilet down the hall and disappeared with a slam of the door. There was never a dull moment with someone as full of surprises as Felix.

While I had not been asleep as long as him, I saw the wisdom in taking advantage of the moment before our reunion turned amorous. I waited a few moments before getting up to wait my turn. It was impossible not to grin when I heard him brushing his teeth.

He startled when he came out and saw me waiting. "Oh my god, did you hear me pee? I'm not sure if I'm ready for that stage of a relationship yet." He scowled when his adorable protest made me almost double over with laughter. "You totally did, didn't you? Damn it, I'm going to die of embarrassment before I get to enjoy my next orgasm."

"Relax, *mon amour*. I gave you your privacy for that. I only heard you brushing your teeth."

"Trust me, you'll thank me for doing that later. I ate a plate of fried onion rings last night because I wasn't expecting anyone would want to make out with me first thing in the morning today."

"I would wish to kiss you even with day-old onion breath."

He snorted at my claim. "Uh-huh. Sure you would. What man in his right mind would choose that over minty fresh?"

"One who is madly in love with you and is grateful he

gets to kiss you at all." I traced his lower lip with my thumb. "Go wait in your room."

He grinned at me. "Ohhhh, so someone decided a pee break was actually a good idea, huh?"

"*Oui*, because once I get you in bed, I am not letting you go again until you have shouted my name as you climax."

Felix swore at my promise as he obeyed.

I took my time in the bathroom to build up his sense of anticipation. When I returned to his room, I was greeted by the arousing sight of him stretching himself open with lubed fingers. "*Mon dieu.*"

He put on a show of preparing himself, causing my prick to twitch as I appreciated the view. His wanton expressions were too much to resist. I positioned myself over him and hungrily kissed him with pent-up desire.

After we parted, he withdrew his fingers as he looked up at me with lust. "I need you inside me, Arsène!"

"What if I wish to worship you slowly instead?" I trailed kisses down his neck as I awaited his answer.

"Soft and gentle sounds great for later. Right now, my ultimate fantasy is you reclaiming me by fucking me hard enough to serve as a reminder of why I should never leave you again. If you *really* want to make my day, pin me facedown and take me with blind, primal lust. Please?"

The desperate plea in his voice made it impossible for me to deny Felix's desires. He was right; there would be plenty of occasions to treat him with tenderness later. If he was after a feral coupling, our time apart was a fantastic incentive to give him what he wanted. "If that is your wish, then get on your knees. I will gladly show you that you are mine, and mine alone."

He got into position on all fours and looked at me over his shoulder with eagerness. "Are you going to punish me for leaving you?"

"Is that what you want most?"

He bit his lower lip as he hesitated to reply. "Is it fucked-up my answer is yes? Because I don't understand why that's what I want, but there's something stupid exciting about the thought of you punishing me in sexy ways. I wouldn't want to be in real trouble, but the fake kind where you get all growly and hold me down—" He cut himself off with a moan.

"Say no more. I will give you what you wish for on one condition."

"That I beg?"

"As long as you understand I am not upset with you for going home. Your family, friends, your entire life is here. I do not resent you for that." He nodded in agreement, which made it easier to consent. "Very well, let us enjoy ourselves to the fullest, eh?"

Felix grinned over his shoulder as he wiggled his ass temptingly. "Come and get me."

Starting off by caressing his sides, I moved them down to spread his cheeks to reveal his pucker. It was wet with lube, and I yearned to bury myself in him once more. "Do you need me to prepare you further?"

"No, I'm good. Please don't hold back."

I rose on my knees to allow me to rub my hardness

against his crack. "Does that mean you wish for me to get rough with you, *mon amour*? Would that please you?"

"Hell yeah. Fuck me up, baby."

I had to bite the inside of my lip to stop myself from laughing at his response. It was hard to pretend to be disciplinarian when he always amused me. Trying to set aside my natural inclination to chuckle at his antics, I did my best to assume the role he wanted me to play. "You will beg me for mercy before I am done with you."

"Will saying 'pretty please' help?"

"You could try it." The most effective method of toying with Felix was to deny him. That was why I took my time sliding into him, savoring his tight heat embracing me on the most intimate level.

He squirmed under me with a huff. "I thought you were supposed to punish me with sexiness."

"What is more punishing than denying you what you want?"

He pouted at me. "Damn it, that's no fun!"

"Patience." I built up to a satisfying rhythm that had him luxuriating under me as he stretched out on the bed.

Knowing his preferences, I dug my fingertips into Felix's soft skin as I gripped his hips. I used my hold to dictate a rough pace as I picked up speed. He was all but mewling under me as I took him hard. It was easy to get caught up in sexual ecstasy, but I focused on my goal.

He reached down to touch himself, but I stopped him from succeeding. "I did not give you permission to pleasure yourself."

"But I need more!"

"Ah, but do you deserve it?"

He keened with frustration when I pinned his arm behind him. "I'm begging you to touch me!"

"It sounds more like you are demanding it, *non*?"

He shoved against me as my hips continued driving into him. In payback, I switched to shallow movements that made him whine low in his throat. "Damn it, I take it back. Being punished sucks. Please fuck me properly."

"If you behave yourself, I will reward you with what you want," I said. "Do you swear to let only me give you what you desire most?"

"Yes, I promise I'll be a good boy if you fuck me like an animal."

I had to stifle my laughter as I released his captured hand. It allowed me to guide him forward to pin him down to the bed face-first with a tight grip on the nape of his neck. "Is this how you want it?"

"Yes, yes, yes!"

Without warning, I began fucking him hard and fast. I kept him on edge by alternating between shallow and deep thrusts. My reward was hearing his cries muffled by the sheets as he rutted against me. It brought out a primitive lust in me that demanded I take everything he offered. My ego purred with satisfaction each time he gasped and moaned fragments of my name, unable to say the whole thing because of the intensity of our coupling.

When I felt him tensing up as he got closer to orgasm, I slowed down the pace.

"No, no, no, no, don't fucking stop!" Felix tried to

force me to resume my earlier rhythm. "Goddamn it, I'm so close!"

Sliding my hand forward, I jerked him up to hold against my body. I lowered my voice to a rumble that made him shudder against me. "You come when I say you do."

A strangled whimper escaped him. "So fucking hot!"

I licked up the sinewy curve of his neck, tasting his sweat. He cried out with lust when I used my teeth to tug on his earlobe. The sound was music to my ears.

Not done teasing him yet, I let my free hand drift down toward his erection, circling the base without making contact. "Do you want me to touch you here?"

"Fucking yes!"

Smirking to myself at what I was about to do, I arrogantly said, "Too bad," then shoved him down to resume pounding into him again.

"Oh, you dick!" His complaint was ruined by how hard he was laughing. "How dare you make that sexy!"

"You are getting rather mouthy, *mon amour*. Perhaps I should spank you for that, hmm?" It was something I was not willing to do without explicit permission.

"Fucking do it!"

I lightly slapped his ass as a test to judge his tolerance level.

Felix hissed as his body jerked under me. "Nope, don't like that at all."

That was all I needed to hear. Caressing him in apology, I promised, "Then I will not do it again."

"Sorry, I got caught up in the moment and thought I'd be into it, but—"

I shushed his concerns. "Do not apologize for changing your mind. That is something I will never punish you for."

"In that case, can I change my mind about one more thing?"

"Of course."

"This is hot as fuck, but I want to see you."

His words filled my heart with warmth. I pulled out of Felix, then helped him turn over to face me. "Like this, or would you rather be on top?"

He spread his legs wider in invitation. "All I need is you inside me, and this will be perfect."

"Do you wish to continue our game?"

He wrapped his arms around my neck in a loose hold. "As much fun as it is getting railed by you as you edge me until I break, I'm dying to get off. Maybe another time?"

"Whenever you desire." I slid back into him with a sigh, feeling complete as our bodies joined as one. Rather than resuming my aggressive pace, I took enormous enjoyment out of making sweet love to him as I caressed him all over.

His body rocked with mine as we gave ourselves over to tender affection until we both climaxed. I leaned forward for a lingering kiss as I basked in the afterglow of our joining. "*Je t'aime, mon amour.* With all of my heart."

"I love you so much." He hugged me tightly. "Please tell me you're staying for a while."

"We can stay here until our appointment this afternoon."

He looked at me with confusion. "What appointment?"

I withdrew and settled next to him. "With Rivena."

He rolled onto his side to face me. "You've lost me. Rivena?"

"She is Rune's Realtor. Since you will one day be living with me, I thought you would like some say on where I move."

His jaw dropped in shock. "Wait, are you serious? You're getting a place out here?"

"*Oui*, and I asked her to make sure our home would have an office for you so you can have your own space to write your books."

Felix pounced on me and started covering me in a flurry of kisses. "I'm so happy, I feel like I could explode into a million rainbows. This is the best thing ever!"

"*Non*, falling in love with you was by far the best thing to happen to me."

"And me." He lifted with a pure joy that filled my soul with light. "As soon as I'm capable of getting it up, I'm giving you the sexiest thank-you of all time."

"I look forward to it."

Felix snuggled on top of me with a cute coo. It was the best feeling in the world to hold him and know he was mine to love forever.

Epilogue

Felix

I dropped onto the couch with a pained groan. My body was screaming complaints after North and I had spent the day packing our apartment so we could move in with our respective boyfriends since our lease was up. "God, even when I'm excited about where I'm going, moving fucking sucks."

North took a seat on our other sofa. "I second that. The only thing that sucks more is *un*packing, ugh. I'm *so* over all this."

His twin, West, came over and made herself comfortable on my lap. Over the past year and a half of living with North, we had become extremely close friends. Much like her brother, she didn't believe in personal boundaries. "I don't know what you're complaining about when I'm the one losing easy access to my beloved Fifi."

I hugged her to make us both feel better. It would be so weird not having her dropping by to visit after I moved in with my boyfriend. "You say that like you'll never see me again. We all know you'll still be stopping by our place all the time."

Arsène sat on the couch arm next to us. "You are most welcome there and at our studio." In the three months he had been in Sunnyside, West's effervescent and quirky personality had charmed him. He had offered to do a photo shoot of her fashion line debut, which had gotten off to an explosive start thanks to their collaboration.

"You're the best, Arsène." West rewarded me with a kiss on the cheek. "Thanks for choosing the best boyfriend in the world. It's so nice I don't have to make his life hell for trying to keep me away from you."

Their mom, Linda, came over to hand out drinks as we waited for Wren and Izzy to get back with our food. She had become a surrogate mother to me, and I adored her as much as if she were my own parent. She spoiled me every time she stopped by to visit or whenever I went over to her house for an Easton family dinner. "Anyone want to take bets on whose place West visits more?"

North snorted at the question as he accepted a drink. "Oh, please. We all know she's going to end up at Felix's way more than mine. She loves him more than me."

We all laughed at that just as Elias returned from using the bathroom and sat down next to North. "What did I miss that was so funny?"

"North was about to declare it a good thing West will visit Felix more, so you'll have more privacy and alone time." Linda smiled as she handed him a soda. It was sweet how much she doted on him and had become a second mother to him, too.

"Yeah, that definitely sounds like a cleaner version of something he'd say."

North wrapped an arm around his boyfriend's shoulders to pull him closer. "Just one of the many reasons I'm happy we're taking the next step in our relationship, minus the moving part, which fucking blows."

Seeing all the boxes in our living room filled me with nostalgia. It was incredible how much everything had changed since I moved in with him at the lowest point in my life after breaking up with Danny. "Man, it's going to be weird not living with you." I accepted a soda when Linda came over, taking a long sip after I opened it.

"Yeah, for sure. But you're not getting rid of me that easily. We'll still hang out all the time and celebrate when your book comes out next year!"

Thanks to Arsène's encouragement, I had finally finished my first full-length novel, *The Prince and His Librarian*. My idea about Prince Leander Montarelli of Maltova and his sarcastic royal librarian, Cyrus Valan, had turned out better than anything I had written before. It was huge that I was actually proud of my work instead of hating it like usual. That didn't stop my fears that no one else would enjoy it, though. "I doubt we'll have a reason to celebrate."

Arsène reached over and stroked my hair. "Nonsense. It will be amazing and worthy of a proper celebration. I have the perfect model in mind for your cover photo. Your book is guaranteed to be a bestseller." My previous boyfriends had made fun of me wanting to be a writer, so it meant the world to me that he cared enough to cheer me on. "I look forward to celebrating by giving you a surprise gift."

"You don't give gifts to failures," I argued. He had been talking up his surprise, but I couldn't let myself get excited about it when I was so convinced that my book would flop.

"Sure they do! It's called a consolation prize," West said. "But there's no way your book is going to fail. It'll be a huge hit."

"They're both right," Linda agreed as she took a seat next to North and Elias. "The draft I read was already amazing. I'm going to be singing your praises to my readers online. I have no doubts about you being at the top of the bestseller list in your genre." Considering she was Arrietty Quenby, one of the most famous fantasy writers in the world, that was an incredible statement. She had insisted on reading my work and had generously helped edit my manuscript and talk me through my trouble spots. Getting a masterclass in writing from someone of her caliber made me count all my lucky stars.

I blushed at the praise. "I'm not ballsy enough to aim that high on my debut book. If people other than my friends and family buy it, I'll be happy."

"They will," Arsène confidently predicted.

Bless him for believing in me. I leaned over to kiss him, which was a challenge with West still on my lap.

Always quick with a joke, Linda chided her daughter. "Honey, if you would get off of Felix, we could all enjoy watching him get properly kissed."

West slid off my lap with a dramatic sigh and a toss of her iridescent rainbow hair. "Fine, I guess that's a sacrifice I can make."

"How noble of you."

Arsène guided me closer and gave me a kiss that

made me wish we were alone—especially once the twins and their mom started catcalling us.

"Oh, I see how it is. We take a load down to the truck so you two can fool around?" Brody asked with his thick Irish brogue and a laugh as he returned with my brother. "Where's dinner?"

"Hopefully with Wren and Izzy on their way back," Elias replied.

Linda wagged her finger at her son. "I could have cooked for everyone if you hadn't packed your kitchen first. You have no one to blame but yourself."

"That won't stop me from blaming Wren and Izzy," he retorted with a smirk. "We'll make it up to you by coming for family dinner next week."

"We will be there, too," Arsène promised, knowing how important she was to me.

West pouted. "I need to find a boyfriend so I don't feel left out when all of you bring your soul mates over on Sunday. It's no fun being the only single one."

"What about Venacio?" I asked. "Or are you still pretending the two of you are friends with benefits, even though we all know that's bullshit?"

She grinned at me. "Do you want to hear all about our sexual exploits in explicit detail? Because if you think Mom being in the room will stop me from gossiping about hooking up with him, I've got a bridge in Brooklyn I can sell you."

North snickered at her claim. "It's insulting you think we believe there's nothing romantic happening with you two."

"Whatever. We're just having fun."

"Lots of naked, sexy fun." I laughed at her wicked smirk.

"And you say you don't love him?" Linda scoffed. "You're lucky denial is a cute look on you."

She beamed at her mom. "Everything is a cute look on me."

"I guess that means that the only ones left to fall in love with each other are Wren and Izzy," I said. "We all know it's just a matter of time."

Arsène chuckled as he stroked his chin. "My brother is not as clueless as he leads Wren to believe. It will be interesting watching that unfold."

"Yeah, like the world's slowest car crash," North joked.

"Hey, either way, it's going to end with a bang, right?" I added with a snicker. Our friends had been dancing around each other flirtatiously as long as I had known them since we met our freshman year. "I hope they return soon."

Almost as if I spoke their arrival into existence, Wren entered with Izzy and carrying several pizzas. We cheered at the sight of food.

"It's about time you're back! I was about to go downstairs to tell you two to stop fooling around in the car while our dinner got cold," North teased them, earning him dual eye rolls.

"Man, it's still weird not having you volunteer to join us in a threesome anymore," Wren said as he set the pizza boxes down on the living room table. He and Izzy each grabbed a slice before sitting on the floor since we were out of space on the couches. "I don't know if I'm ever going to get used to that."

"It's your fault for missing out when you had the chance. I'm too in love with Elias to even think such things now." North leaned over and gave his boyfriend a kiss.

"Bullshit," Wren said through a fake cough, causing us all to laugh while poor Elias blushed like a cherry tomato. "Or are you going to tell us your threesome fantasies only involve Elias and his identical twin? Because that's pretty kinky, and I'm kinda into it, not gonna lie."

North's wolfish grin caused Elias to hide his face with an embarrassed noise, earning him a sympathetic pat on the head by Linda sitting next to him. "I'm sorry, honey. You're just too damn cute for your own good."

"Yeah, he is," North agreed. "Speaking of kinky and threesomes, where are Rune and Callum? Shouldn't they be here by now?"

Izzy gave him a disapproving look. "When you use that kind of segue, it reveals a lot about you that you should probably keep to yourself."

North laughed as he handed Elias a slice of cheese pizza before grabbing a pepperoni one for himself. "Oh, please. There isn't a single person in this room who hasn't fantasized about getting fucked by Rune in an elevator at least once."

"Callum texted me that Rune's meeting with his manager ran a little late, but they're on their way." I leaned over and took a slice of pepperoni pizza. "Giving Rune the courtesy of pretending we're not all a bunch of perverts lusting after him is the least we can do for making us so many awesome desserts. Besides, it's twice as inappropriate now that they're engaged." Rune had proposed to Callum two weeks ago after returning from a work trip to Italy with a custom-made bow tie. North's inappropriate comments aside, we were all so happy for them.

"That's fine. Teasing Wren and Izzy about when they're going to make it official between them is way more fun, anyway."

Izzy arched one delicate eyebrow. "You make it sound like I have to submit formal paperwork to officially be his friend."

Wren pretended to act aghast. "You mean you haven't submitted your friendship forms in triplicate yet? Aw man, our friendship is going to be declared illegal if you don't do it soon."

A smile tugged at the corner of Izzy's mouth as he attempted to hide his amusement at his best friend's antics. "Knowing it's forbidden would make a friendship with me more alluring, *non*?"

"I think by 'friendship,' you mean 'romance,'" North corrected him, using air quotes for good measure.

Wren shook his head. "Yeah, right. If I tried to be romantic with Iz, he would laugh himself into oblivion at my pathetic attempts at wooing him."

"And how exactly would you woo me?" he asked with an interested hum.

"I'm pretty sure sneaking into your room naked won't do it. I mean, I'm down to try it, but—"

"Did you learn that technique from North?"

"In my defense, I've had outstanding success with that in the past," North said with a smirk. "You could do worse."

Wren finished his pizza slice before asking, "Would you prefer a bed of roses and some candles?"

Augie made a face at the suggestion. "Trust me, you don't want to do that. Cleaning it up is a pain and if you knock over a candle, it's all over. Nobody's attempts at romancing should involve the fire department."

I grinned at my brother. "That sure sounds like you're speaking from experience. Did Brody's anniversary surprise have a fiery mishap that you forgot to tell me about?"

"No, he explicitly forbade me from using flower petals of any kind in the bed and absolutely no candles," Brody denied. "I'm lucky he allowed me to take him to a cabin with a fireplace."

There was another knock on the door, and this time Callum and Rune entered, setting off a chorus of hellos. When the rest of us were in blue jeans and T-shirts, the two of them were overdressed in stylish suits, with Callum pairing his with a cute pink argyle bow tie. Rune was sexy as sin itself in his black suit, with a silver shirt that made his icy blue eyes even more hypnotic than usual. It took a concentrated effort not to let my overactive imagination perv out over a fantasy about him and Arsène when they were both in the same room. Arsène may be my boyfriend, but their combined sexiness was too much for my gutter-brain.

"I apologize for my meeting running long and delaying us," Rune said.

"We got here as fast as we could," Callum added. "Is there still pizza left?"

I gestured to the boxes on the coffee table. "Yep, help yourself! Glad you could make it."

"Did we miss anything?"

"Oh, you know. Just the usual teasing Izzy and Wren they're one playful disagreement away from tearing off each other's clothes and going at it like rabbits," North said.

"If that's your reason for leaving wet towels in the bathroom, you can stop doing that," Izzy told Wren. "Being a slob won't get my attention."

"Well, if that and getting naked in your bed isn't, what is?"

Izzy gave him a flirty smile. "You'll just have to be creative."

"If you need ideas, Felix and I have a million of them," North offered. "I'm sure between the three of us, Wren, we can come up with the perfect method of seducing your haughty prince."

"He wouldn't even know what to do with me if I said yes to him."

Wren lit up with an excited look. "Oh, game on, Iz. I can never resist a good challenge."

We all continued joking and talking while finishing dinner. In some ways, moving out seemed like the end of an era. However, as I looked up at Arsène with a smile, I couldn't wait to spend the rest of our lives together in love.

Thank you for reading **Picture Love**! Want to see more of Felix and Arsène? A bonus chapter called "Naked Thank-You" is available to my newsletter subscribers. It also includes a visual guide. To read it, visit my website at www.afzoelle.com to sign up and download it!

Next up is **Love Practice**! You definitely won't want to miss Wren and Izzy's hilarious and steamy friends to lovers, roommates, fake dating romance. These two have simmering sexual chemistry that's just waiting to explode, so give it a read and fall in love with them.

Thank You

THANK YOU FOR READING *Picture Love*. I love hearing from readers, so please consider leaving a review and letting everyone know how much you enjoyed it.

Reviews are crucial for helping new readers discover me and decide whether or not they want to take a chance on my books. If you could take a moment to share your thoughts, I'd really appreciate it!

Recommending my work to others is also a huge help, so if you liked this book, please consider spreading the word to others!

About the Series

If you want to see more of Felix and Arsène's story, you can read an exclusive extra epilogue if you **join my newsletter**.

If this was your first book in the **Good Bad Idea** series, you should check out **Bet on Love** to see where all the fun begins.

The seventh and final book of this series is **Love Practice**. It focuses on Izzy and Wren's romance, two best friends and roommates who have an intense sexual chemistry just waiting to explode. After failing to get a second date too many times, Wren asks Izzy to be his dating tutor. It involves going on practice dates, which Izzy secretly hopes will teach Wren how to love only him. It's a sexy, funny, and heartfelt friends to lovers, roommates, fake dating romance that will make you laugh and hit you right in the feels in all the best ways.

Since it's the final book in the **Good Bad Idea** series, most of the characters appear to wrap things up. It'll be a fitting sendoff for this series which has changed so much for me.

For those of you who were fans of Armand, I'm happy to announce that he'll be starring in his own book called **Changerous Liaisons** in my next series, **Suite Dreams**. It features couples who fall in love at Luxurian Hotels around the world. That also means that the

Good Bad Idea guys will be putting in cameo appearances, so that's something to look forward to!

To stay up to date on the latest series news, please be sure to subscribe to my newsletter, follow me on Twitter, or join my Facebook group, A.F. Zoelle's Amazing AF Readers. I do exclusive previews every Teaser Tuesday and WIP Wednesday, so please come join us if you want a glimpse at what I'm working on for the future.

Next in Series

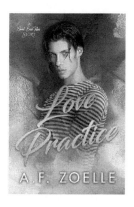

Wren is kinda sorta super in love with his best friend. Asking Izzy to go on practice dates as his dating tutor probably isn't the best idea to keep those feelings hidden. But a bad idea's never stopped Wren before.

WREN FERRES

DOES ANYONE KNOW HOW to make Prince Charming fall in love with you? I'm asking for a friend.

...yeah, that friend is me. I'm secretly a little in love with my best friend and roommate. Okay, I'm a *lot* in love with him. Like, truly, madly, *deeply* in love with him. But it's not my fault! He's hot, French, and laughs at all my stupid jokes. He's the prince of my dreams, minus the part where he isn't actual royalty and not in love with me.

Determined to change that, I come up with a brilliant plan to challenge Monsieur Know-it-all to be my dating tutor. I'm hoping that'll tempt him into acting on our flirtatious banter.

If it doesn't, maybe I'll push my luck by suggesting some kissing practice?

ISIDORE "IZZY" DEVEREAUX

Wren is flirty, quirky, *très* cute—and completely oblivious about how much I love him. His wild ideas usually make me laugh, but his request to go on practice dates to give him pointers? Yeah, that pushes all my buttons. Agreeing to his outlandish request means risking him discovering my secret. But, it also presents a tempting opportunity. This is my one chance to make him see me as more than just his best friend. It could be my only shot at making him my boyfriend for real.

I may not be a real prince like he teases me about, but can't we still have a happily ever after?

Love Practice is the seventh and final book in the ***Good Bad Idea*** series and part of the Sunnyside universe. This novel features a friends to lovers, roommates, fake dating romance. Full of cute sweetness and sexy fun, every story ends with a satisfying HEA and no cliffhangers. Each book can be read as a standalone or as part of the series in order.

Also by A.F. Zoelle

For a complete and up-to-date list of A.F. Zoelle's releases, please visit her website at

www.afzoelle.com

GOOD BAD IDEA SERIES

Bet on Love

Love Means More

Fancy Love

Love Fool

Love Directions

Picture Love

Love Practice

ILLICIT ILLUSIONS SERIES

Alluring Attraction

Developing Desires

Embracing Euphoria

SUITE DREAMS SERIES

Snowbody Like You

Acknowledgements

It is such a relief to finally get to share Felix and Arsène's story with you all. I hope that they have stolen your hearts the same way they did mine. Everything about this book has been a joy, especially having so many people share in their happiness.

One of the best parts of 2020 was getting to become friends with so many of my readers. Amy Mitchell and Niki Cosgrove are not only amazing beta readers, but they have both become close friends who mean so much to me. Lindsay Porter and Tammy Jones have also touched my heart with the passion they've shared with me.

I'm also endlessly grateful to the amazing Quinn Ward, who has been an incredible mentor and friend to me. Their guidance and encouragement have helped me grow as an author and they make me feel like I can shoot for the moon.

Pam and Sandra continue to be the best people to work with and I thank my lucky stars that I get to work with them.

I also am so thankful for Katie from Gay Romance Reviews and all of the ARC readers who have been so kind and encouraging! Their efforts have helped so many people discover me, for which I am endlessly appreciative.

I can't wait to meet again in **Love Practice**!

About the Author

WWW.AFZOELLE.COM

Under constant siege from persistent plot bunnies, A.F. Zoelle enjoys humoring them by writing about gorgeous men being in love. Her contemporary romances are full of witty banter, sexy fun, and lovable smart-asses. She's left academia behind for a new adventure, which will hopefully include adopting Ragdoll cats of her own someday soon.

For more information on new releases and access to exclusive content, sign up for A.F. Zoelle's newsletter. To subscribe, visit her website at www.afzoelle.com.

You can also join her Facebook Group, A.F. Zoelle's Amazing AF Readers, at www.facebook.com/groups/amazingafzoelle, or follow her on Twitter @af_zoelle.

Made in the USA
Middletown, DE
21 April 2021